WHO'S THAT WITCH?

A WITCHES OF HOLIDAY HILLS COZY MYSTERY

CAROLYN RIDDER ASPENSON

WHO'S THAT WITCH?

For Cooper, the best cat ever
See you at the Rainbow Bridge
LUMI

1

M y apartment lit up like a Christmas tree on steroids. My Amazon Echo burst to life, playing "Lyin' Eyes" by the Eagles so loud I couldn't hear myself think. I shot up in my bed, instantly on high alert as I rubbed the shock from my eyes. "What the blazes?"

Cooper had already jumped at least two feet in the air from the bottom of my bed, the noise waking him from a sound sleep too. "Where's the party?" He crawled to the side of the bed and examined the outside through the cracks of my blinds. "Are we at Mardi Gras?" He stared at me, his teeny cat voice competing with the music. "Where are your beads? You need beads in this town."

I should have rolled my eyes, but I was a little stunned by the lights and music and being awakened from the perfect dream filled with puppies and Ryan Reynolds. "No, we're not in New Orleans. We're home. In bed."

Mr. Charming squawked in the corner of my room. "The end is near," he screeched. "The end is near!"

The lights flickered, dimming to a soft glow as the song dialed down to a murmur.

"Oh, my bad." Cooper climbed up on my pillow and sniffed me carefully. "You okay?"

I nodded. "What do you think that was?"

"Meh, don't know. Probably a power surge."

"In the middle of the night? How much power are people using while they're sleeping?" I climbed out of bed and peeked out my window. The streetlights flickered and finally cut off. I glanced at my old clock radio—I kept the thing because some life savers should never go out of style —and watched it flash 12:02 a.m. Of course, it wasn't 12:02 a.m., and I knew this because I went to bed at 12:15.

Cooper meowed through a downward kitty stretch. "Let me see what's going on." He crawled to my bedroom door and did a cursory examination of our small apartment. "Looks like everything's okay." He sauntered back into bed and nuzzled into the pillows next to mine. "I'm goin' with power surge for the win." Within seconds, tiny snores hummed from his nose.

"Ugh." I stared at him with raised eyebrows. "How do you do that?" I fluffed my pillow, then dropped my head on it and waited for sweet slumber to return. But it didn't. My mind relaxed some, but my gut told me that wasn't a simple power surge.

And whatever it was, I needed to be ready.

"JUST MOVE YOUR FOOT."

I cringed. "No. His claws are like vise grips. It'll hurt."

"Slowly. Move it slowly," Cooper said.

"No," I repeated. "I'm scared."

My familiar shook his little cat head. "Abby, you can't stand like that forever."

"Tell that to Mr. Charming. He's the one whose claws are crushing my head."

"Go ahead, make my day," Mr. Charming said.

Gabe snickered while Bessie flat-out laughed.

I narrowed my eyes at them, but I was secretly laughing a little inside. How many witches have talking parrots with a freakish obsession with Clint Eastwood? Just one. Me. Okay, technically two, because Mr. Charming recently became Bessie's familiar, but he struggled with letting go of me. I reminded him of my deceased mother. It was hard to be upset about that because I also felt connected to him for that very same reason.

Needless to say, his obsession with the iconic actor was hilarious. I'd been stuck standing with a green parrot on top of my head, his claws of life digging into my scalp every time I shifted even a centimeter. And each time I tried, he squawked and said, "Go ahead, make my day."

Seriously. I can't make this stuff up.

"You're going to have to magically remove him," Bessie said.

"Uh, no. That's mean. You know how familiars feel about being manipulated by magic. I don't want to upset him."

Bessie and Gabe rolled their eyes.

"Come on! You know how it works. You use magic on your familiar and they lose faith in you. I can't do that to Mr. Charming."

"Go ahead, make my day," the parrot said, doing his best Clint impression yet.

I exhaled. "Or maybe I can."

"It shouldn't be a problem. He's not your familiar," Bessie said.

"Glad someone knows that," my actual familiar said.

I glanced down at Cooper and cringed, then glanced back up at Bessie. "I know that, but you asked me to watch him last night, and I did. And you know we have a connection." I groaned. "Can't you make him move?"

"Using magic on a familiar creates a lack of trust," she said with a smile.

Gabe and Cooper laughed.

I gave Gabe the evil eye. "Some boyfriend you are."

"Ouch," he said, but his smile showed he wasn't at all hurt.

"Bird-sitting is one thing, but this bird needs psychological treatment if he thinks he's got two witches to protect. Maybe he's doing this to get back at me? I had to finish inventory. He doesn't like it when I work late," Bessie said.

I stayed perfectly still. "Ya think?"

"I told you watching *Sudden Impact* was a mistake," Gabe said.

He was right. "But he loves that movie, and you know how much he's been through lately."

"I love tuna, but I don't see you going out of your way to please me," Cooper said.

"Oh please." I gave him the biggest eye roll I could muster without having the claws of life rip my long hair. Parrots, like babies, are a valid reason for updos, my mother always said. She was right. She was always right.

Bessie had enough. "None of us have time for this." She held out her arm, waved her hand in a half-moon shape, and said, "Birds of prey do not obey. Birds with love need a little shove." She flicked her hand again, and Mr. Charming flew to her arm and perched there. She smiled at his sweet face. "Hey, sweetie."

"How come he's not mad?" I asked.

"I guess he just loves me more," she said.

He turned to me. "Nobody—I mean nobody—puts ketchup on a hotdog."

Gabe coughed.

I stomped my foot on the ground. "I don't do that!"

Cooper rubbed up against my leg. "Time to go back to Disney movies."

"Right," I said. "Because that's what we need. Disney parents dying and animals or people in crisis. That'll make the bird happy again."

Bessie handed Mr. Charming a blackberry. He munched it down quickly. "He's a big sweetie. You have to stop stressing him out with violence on TV."

Clearly, she hadn't watched Disney in a while. "Yes, ma'am." I glanced at Gabe, my sexy, law-enforcing, newly appointed significant-other warlock.

He pressed his lips together but failed miserably at not smiling.

"Anyway," I said as I moved toward my regular table to begin my daily writing. "What's on your agenda today?"

Neither Gabe nor Bessie spoke.

I pointed to Gabe. "You. I'm asking you."

"Oh." His lips curved upward, and a little sparkle flashed in his eyes. "Solving crimes and kicking butt like a police chief does."

"Only that's not your real job," I said.

"It's a job. It's just not my main job."

Not only was Gabe the Holiday Hills chief of police, but he was also a very successful investigator for the MBI, the Magical Bureau of Investigations. Magicals who worked for the MBI traveled the world working hard to preserve magic and maintain its integrity. Prior to believing in witches, I wrote a cozy mystery series featuring a witch who worked for a similar organization. I just never knew it was a real thing.

I opened my laptop and plugged in the charger. "Any big cases lately?"

He raised his left brow.

"I know. I'm not supposed to ask." I shrugged. "Sue me."

Bessie chuckled and took her familiar back into the kitchen. "Time to make the donuts," she said as she walked through the door.

Stella burst into the store, sweat glistening on her temples. "You are not going to believe what I just saw!"

Bessie peeked back out from behind the kitchen door. "What happened?"

Stella dropped her bag on the floor and caught her breath.

Bessie and Mr. Charming came back in to get the scoop.

"She needs a minute," I said.

"Every day for the past ten years, Loretta there's been giving me a large black coffee. Today she gives me a large black coffee, only it has sugar in it, a lotta sugar," Mr. Charming said.

"Good grief," I said.

Stella tilted her head to the left. "What's wrong with the bird?"

Gabe crossed his arms over his chest. "He watched *Sudden Impact* again last night."

Stella narrowed her eyes at Bessie, who waved her arms in front of her. "Blame your best friend. She had him for the night."

Stella shook off the crazy, then plopped into a chair at my desk. Okay, technically it was a table and belonged to Bessie, but it was the one I used daily as my work desk.

"Something crazy is happening in this town. The bird is proof."

"Did you have another one of those online dates?" Bessie asked.

"No, ma'am, worse. I just saw a broomstick sweeping the sidewalk."

"That's what they're designed to do," I said.

"No one was holding it."

The hairs on the back of my neck stood. I glanced quickly at Cooper, whose teeny eyes widened enough for me to see his entire pupil. I made eye contact with Bessie and Gabe, hoping my facial expression wasn't as obvious as theirs.

Cooper spoke, but thankfully Stella just heard the meows of a cranky cat. "Well, crap. Sounds like the word's out. Guess we might as well load up on the tuna now before the world freaks out and stockpiles it like it's toilet paper."

I had no clue how to respond to that.

Bessie finished making Stella a cup of tea. I wondered if it included a magical herb, maybe one to help her forget the magically sweeping broom, but after she sipped it and continued talking, I realized it was just regular old tea.

"I think I'm losing my mind."

"You aren't losing your mind." I cupped my hand over hers. "It's probably one of the Halloween tricks Holiday Hills is famous for doing."

"It's February."

"Sometimes people here like to mess with others and leave them out longer. You know that."

Bessie nodded. "Two years ago they kept that ghost in Victoria Longley's old boutique, the one that new owner Cassie renamed Vintage Mass. Every time someone opened the door, the ghost swooped down and skirted across the entranceway. Old Mr. Reynolds had to wear Depends every time he went there with his wife." She shook her head and giggled. "And he always waited outside."

"Poor Mr. Reynolds. He was a sweet man," I said. We lost him a few years ago, and Holiday Hills went into mourning. Granted, the town did that every time we lost someone, because everyone is special in Holiday Hills.

"I know," Stella said. "And that's the first thing I thought, but it was just so real, you know?" She tipped the teacup to her lips and sipped the luscious lavender-scented drink. "I even looked for fishing string, but I didn't see any." She took another sip of tea. "I think I need a vacation."

"Ditto that," I said. After the midnight light display and impromptu Eagles concert, I meant it.

It was just past seven-thirty on Monday morning, and the new Enchanted regulars arrived for their morning coffee klatch. A while back we had other regulars, but the magical world is ever-changing, not to mention full of angst, and they're no longer among us. The chairs sat empty for quite some time until Bessie finally tossed them and purchased new-to-her ones from an antique store in Dahlonega, Georgia. Their dark, cushiony, leather-covered seats were perfect for relaxing and enjoying a good book and a cup of coffee. Thankfully, the new chairs brought in more customers, and new regulars.

The Enchanted, Bessie's life's work, was a bookstore until it became a bookstore with coffee and sometimes sandwiches Bessie made in the back for her favorite customers. Word got out about her turkey club, and just last month the renovations were completed. Bessie finally celebrated her grand reopening of the Enchanted Books Café. She'd been so busy she hired a part-time employee, a sweet young high-school warlock named Atlas Spencer. Atlas came in every morning at five o'clock to prep for the morning rush, then showed up after school for the afternoon. His curly blond hair and blue eyes topped off a tall, lean, muscular seventeen-year-old physique that brought the high-school girls by daily for swooning, flirtatious competitions. She hadn't done the math, but I suspected Bessie's daily sales increased five-fold, if that's an actual fold, because of Atlas. He was a cutie—for the high-school girls, that is. For my age group, he was cute like a little brother who might have had a crush on your friends. But they didn't make boys like that in my day. My generation lucked out—and I say that with complete sarcasm—with the grunge-era leftovers who wore their pants with the waist at the knees and dingy T-shirts their mommas refused to wash. I wasn't quite sure any of them showered in high school. They'd progressed to man buns and long beards, two things a lot of women liked, but I wasn't one of them. I liked a clean-cut, masculine man with short hair and broad shoulders. Men, or warlocks, like Gabe. And I knew for a fact that Gabe would never wear his hair long enough to put in a bun. Thank you, Goddess, for that.

Atlas also seemed to have a bit of a thing for Stella, like a wishful Mrs. Robinson thing, though that wouldn't happen in this lifetime. Stella thought he was a cutie too, but there was no way my best friend would do that. *Ew.*

Poor kid tried to hide his interest, but when she was around, he blushed and choked on most of what he said. It was adorable. Thankfully, Stella hadn't noticed, and I didn't want to embarrass him further by telling her. Stella is the kind of woman men drool over, yet she never pays attention.

The new regulars were three magicals: Mr. Waylon Hastings, Mr. James Calloway, and Mr. Roger Jameson. Mr. Hastings and Mr. Jameson were warlocks, but Mr. Calloway was a shifter. I admit he made me nervous, but only because of his supernatural status. Some might consider that magical profiling or even prejudice, but I don't care. My experience with shifters has been touchy, and my feelings take precedence for me. I have to stop letting past issues get in the way of my life, but until I can, it's just the way I am.

The café's former regulars had shifters in the mix, and let's just say my life wasn't easy because of them. In fact, my life wasn't easy back then at all. I'd recently lost my mom and discovered I was a magical instead of a human, and learned the world included things I'd only ever written about. Things like shifters, witches, warlocks, talking cats, and brooms that flew by themselves.

Witches, by the way, never fly on brooms. That's the stuff of fairytales.

Suffice it to say, learning I'm a witch has been a major life adjustment.

Gabe kissed my forehead. "I hate to drink and leave, but I've got a new detective coming on board this morning, and I've got to organize his paperwork."

I blew him a kiss. "I'll see you tonight?"

"Can I get back to you? I may take him to dinner."

I nodded. Gabe worked two full-time jobs, and I had a feeling his new hire did also. If he spent the evening with him, that meant not only had my boyfriend hired a new detective for the Holiday Hills Police Department, but likely for his supernatural job too.

After a recent situation involving myself and a not-so-good witch, I'd been asked to work with the MBI. Gabe pressed the issue, but I decided that instead of investigating witches, I'd much rather write paranormal cozy mysteries about them. My newest novel is the first in my series with my own name—usually, I work as a ghostwriter. I'm a *USA*

Today Bestselling author, but I don't get credit for it. I'm lucky my publisher knows my writing and immediately contracted me to write my new series, The Adelle Arden Paranormal Mystery Series, which honors my mom.

"If Gabe can't make it tonight, I could use a girls' night," Stella said. "Minus the mysterious self-sweeping brooms, please."

"I can handle that," I said, then chuckled. "No pun intended."

"On that note." Gabe rotated on his heels and pointed to the door. "I'm outta here."

Stella and Bessie laughed.

STELLA GIGGLED when I slammed my MacBook closed. "Are you sure you don't want me to read it?"

Stella's the best editor I know, and there are times when we work great together, but other times we use those opportunities to channel our inner demons and allow them to express their angst. It can get ugly. Five books ago I asked her to read a chapter for me. I wanted to make sure the secrets were revealed but not just as bullet points I laid out for the readers. I'd read and reread the chapter, changing it up each time, but something was off, and I just wasn't happy with it. She promised to give it a read-through and be honest. And boy, was she. She said I'd word vomited the secrets and all I was missing were those bullet points.

Word vomited.

Okay, so I'm not one of those high-maintenance diva writers you read about on the internet, I promise, but no author likes to hear she's word vomited anything. If I didn't love her so much, I would have turned her into a toad. Witches do that. Trust me.

"I'm good."

She fixed her eyes on mine. "I said I'm sorry."

"For what?" I asked, as if I didn't already know.

Word vomit sat heavy like an elephant in the chair between us.

"Don't make me say it. I was having a bad day when I read it. I swear."

I didn't look at her, because if I did, I'd smile and ruin her never-ending apology.

She threw her hands in the air. "Fine! I'll give you Andrew Walker if you let me help you, and I promise not to be a jerk."

"Hmm." My eyes sparkled. "I do love Andrew, but I think I'd prefer Kristoffer Polaha now."

"What? You're kidding, right?"

I stared at her with no expression. "Does this look like the face of someone who's kidding?"

She groaned. "Fine, I won't read it."

"Wow. I see a Hallmark boyfriend is more important than your best friend's work. Nice." I laid it on thick because it was fun.

Stella and I, probably the biggest Hallmark fans in the entire universe, claimed our movie boyfriends and declared them off the market. The problem was, the longer we were friends, the more similar our tastes in men became. She'd claimed Polaha a few years back, when I wasn't interested, but lately that's changed. I'm not afraid to work those boyfriends into negotiations, but it was impossible—Stella had locked them up in her imaginary boyfriend cage and thrown away the key.

Bessie walked by laughing. "You two and those movie actors. Like any of them would come to Holiday Hills."

"Clint Eastwood was here just a few minutes ago," I said.

She shook her head and laughed again.

Cooper chimed in. "Shoot for a can of salmon and call it even." Cooper had always obsessed over tuna, but he'd recently added salmon to his list when Bessie gave him some fresh stuff she'd used for bagels. She'd also spoiled him with anchovies. I'd yet to forgive her for that. The smell of those things lingered for days.

"It's fine," I said. I smiled at Stella, deciding to cut her some slack on the fake-boyfriend thing. "I just need a break. Adelle is pushing the story to go one way, and I want it to go another."

"I hate it when the characters come to life like that."

"Especially when those characters are a younger fictional version of your own mother who says words like 'babe' and 'tasty.'"

Stella cringed. "Ew. That's wrong on every level."

"Right? Trust me, I'm not doing it intentionally. The character just does her own thing."

"That's what all writers say."

"Trust me, it's true."

Cassie Mayflower walked in, pulling her long brown-and-black scarf from her neck as the door closed behind her. She fluffed out her shoulder-length black hair from under her coat and smiled at us. "Hey, y'all!" Cassie's from Massachusetts but likes to pretend she's a born-and-bred Southerner, even though her northeastern accent is obvious. "How's it going?"

Bessie caught my eye and raised her eyebrows. She didn't dislike Cassie Mayflower, but she didn't exactly like her either.

"Hey, Ms. Mayflower," Stella said. "I walked by your place earlier. That broomstick scared me to death!"

I watched the older witch with intent.

"What do you mean?" Cassie asked.

"The broomstick that sweeps itself. I couldn't find any string attached to it. Is it remote-powered or something?"

Cassie pursed her lips. "I'm not sure what you're talking about."

I spoke before Stella had the chance. "She's talking about that broom. You know, the one that's connected to the invisible wire and sweeps without someone holding it?"

Cassie blinked and glanced at Bessie for help.

Bessie nodded once. "You mentioned something about that the other day."

"Oh, that!" Cassie made a big deal out of acting like she'd done it. She waved her hand and then tossed her big black purse onto the counter. "Goddess be, I completely forgot I'd left that thing up. I'll have to check on it when I go into the boutique in a bit."

"You...you should keep it up," I said. "You know, so other people can freak about it too. It's funny." My eyes pleaded with hers, then Bessie's. "Right, Bessie?"

She nodded. "Of course. Practical jokes are fun." It would have been believable if she'd had a little fun in her tone when she said it.

Cassie smiled at my best friend. "Stella, come on by after ten, and I'll treat you to a new hand moisturizer. I'm sure your hands are dry as sandpaper in this weather."

Actually, unlike the dry, cold winters in Massachusetts, North Georgia winters were wet from too much rain, but that didn't mean it was warm. Warm wasn't a universal feeling. Southerners didn't adjust as easily to winter as northeastern people did, so while forty degrees in the northeast allowed for sweatshirts or sweaters and no coats, here in the South we bundled up with down-filled jackets until it warmed up even more. Gas heat dried our skin just like it did in the colder states, and a good moisturizer always helped.

"Oh, I'd love a new moisturizer," Stella said. She loved herself a freebie.

"Bessie, can we chat privately for a moment?" Cassie asked. "Outside would be lovely."

Bessie nodded, finished preparing Cassie's coffee, and led her outside.

"Have a great day, Ms. Mayflower," I hollered.

"Honey, Ms. Mayflower is my former mother-in-law, and a nasty old biddy at that. Please, call me Cassie."

"Cassie it is," I said.

The door closed behind them and then quickly reopened. By itself. Stella's eyes widened, so I swooped my hand in a tight loop beside me, hoping she didn't see. I'd created a wind effect that pushed the door open again and made a howling sound as it pulled closed.

"Wow, it sure is windy this morning," she said.

"Seems to be," I said.

"At first I thought the door opened and closed by itself."

"It's because the broomstick freaked you out."

"It didn't freak me out. It surprised me and scared me. I swear there's no wire or string or anything attached to that thing."

"Stella, it's a leftover Halloween joke."

"You think I'm crazy."

"No, I think you got spooked and you're coming off the adrenaline from it."

"I saw a broom sweeping by itself."

"It's just a silly Halloween trick."

"A week past Valentine's Day."

"True, but you're not crazy. Well, I mean, yeah, you're crazy, but in a good way."

She smiled. "I love how you get me."

Of course I got her. What I didn't get was why strange things were happening in my comfy, quiet little town.

2

S tella had a Zoom call with her new client, so after preparing for an hour, she headed back to her apartment for the meeting. I breathed a sigh of relief. I loved Stella, but sometimes she liked to chat more than I had time for. Books don't write themselves, and as an editor who creates deadlines for people like me, she should know that.

She probably does, but doesn't care.

The new regulars were still arguing about football from forty years ago while sipping their third cups of coffee, so I meandered over for some opinions, but not about sports. Sports weren't my thing, and no matter how hard I tried to like them, I just didn't.

"Gentlemen," I said, smiling at the group.

Waylon Hastings's eyes lit up and a smile stretched across his face. "Why, Miss Odell, don't you look lovely today?"

Roger Jameson grunted. "Way, you've been gawking at her for over an hour now. Don't act like you didn't know she was here."

Mr. Hastings admitted he had a harmless crush on me. But only because I reminded him of his late wife, he swore, when she was my age. He'd been a widow for several years now, and the community was glad he was finally venturing out in public on a regular basis. "She reminds me of my wife, you old—" He waved his hand. "Whatever you are." Mr. Hastings had a bit of a memory problem, poor soul. No one liked to talk about it.

"A gentle soul is what I am, you old coot."

Well, I could sense where this was going, and while it was excellent fodder for my story, I needed their input. "Gentlemen, did you notice the door opening a little bit ago?"

Mr. Hastings nodded.

"Did you think it was odd?" I asked.

He shrugged. "Figured it was the wind. Nothing weird about the wind opening a door now and then."

"I thought it was odd," Mr. Calloway said.

Mr. Jameson nodded. "Thought so too. Why are you asking?"

"It's not windy out," I said. "The second time it opened, I created the wind. The first time it just opened, no wind involved."

"It's raining. We always get a bit of wind in February when it rains," Mr. Jameson said.

"He's right," Mr. Calloway said.

"How would you know?" Mr. Hastings asked. "You're usually hibernating about now."

"Yet here I sit, wasting my time with you."

I smiled. Even though I wasn't entirely comfortable with Mr. Calloway's true self, I did enjoy his sense of humor. His true self is a black bear, and they normally do hibernate in the winter, but Georgia bears usually don't.

The weather never gets cold enough, messing up their internal clock.

"You think it's something else?" Mr. Jameson asked.

I sat in the empty chair across from him. Cooper wandered over and planted himself between my feet, studying the three men as if he would eat them given the chance. I wouldn't put it past him. He had some serious food quirks.

I chose not to mention what happened the night before, but I found it odd they hadn't brought it up. In fact, no one had. I hadn't had the chance to talk about it with Bessie or Gabe because Mr. Charming latched onto me the moment I got out of bed, and by the time he released me from his clawed prison, I'd forgotten about it. If no one mentioned it, did that mean it had been for my benefit only? "Stella said she saw a broom sweeping on its own outside Cassie Mayflower's boutique this morning."

Mr. Jameson set down his coffee and picked up a copy of the local paper. "Probably just a leftover trick from some human who thinks magic ain't real."

"Did you happen to see the lights outside in the middle of the night? It was like someone turned on every light outside the main area of town."

"I slept like a rock last night," Mr. Calloway said.

"I'm with him. Sleeping is my favorite thing to do these days," Mr. Jameson added.

I glanced at Mr. Hastings. "Can't say I saw it either."

"Well, it happened. Then the door whipping open and Stella seeing the broom sweeping by itself? Seems fishy to me."

"Could be a flux in the system," Mr. Hastings said.

"What's a flux?" Mr. Calloway asked.

That's what I wanted to know.

"For humans, it's the process of wind blowing in or out, or if you're a human doctor, it's an abnormal discharge of blood or other human fluid from the body," Mr. Hastings replied.

"I haven't had my breakfast yet," Mr. Calloway said.

"You asked," Mr. Hastings shot back.

"You should have given me a spoiler before going all in like that," Mr. Calloway said.

I felt the shifter's pain. My stomach lurched at the mention of *other human stuff*, setting my writer's creative mind off on a tangent. "So, for magicals, it could be what? A shift in the magical air?"

"Seems about right," Mr. Hastings said.

"That doesn't sound good."

"I'm inclined to agree with you."

Mr. Jameson scooted toward me and whispered, "You know he's got the issues?" He pointed to his temple. "Don't listen to the warlock."

Atlas rushed out from the kitchen. "I'm so busted!" He grabbed his backpack from under the counter and bolted out the door.

"Well," Bessie said as she came inside, "looks like we lost track of time again, and he's missed first period already."

I checked my watch. "And part of second period, unless they've changed school hours."

"I need to set a timer from now on."

"Sounds like you do," I said.

A booming crack of thunder followed by a colossal bolt of lightning shook the building. The ceiling lights burst, and the fire alarm went off before the entire place went dark.

"Well, time to head home." Mr. Hastings flicked his hand and disappeared.

I magically acquired a flashlight and lit up the café, smiling at Mr. Hastings still standing there.

"Oh dear, I thought I was home," he said, and then he disappeared for real.

"Bessie," I whispered. "Did you see the lights on last night?"

"The lights? I thought that was a dream?"

"Do witches dream the same dreams?"

"If so, I've never experienced it."

"Ditto. Gabe didn't mention seeing any lights," I said.

"Neither did Stella."

"What does that mean?"

"I'm not sure, but I gather you want to find out."

"That's an understatement."

"I have no doubt you'll figure it out, then."

"I wouldn't be so sure."

"Oh, sweetie, I am. You're a powerful witch, dear. You can do anything."

MAYBE MR. HASTINGS, memory issues aside, was right. Maybe there was some weird flux in the magical world. If so, that would be detrimental to magicals. Stella had experienced a magical event, and that never happened. Magicals lived among humans, but magic was our secret. Humans didn't see what we did, and when something magical happened, they didn't experience it.

Still, our worlds couldn't mix. People like Stella would lose their minds, and Goddess only knew what kind of havoc the two worlds joining would wreak. I needed a break from Adelle and her refusal to follow my outline, and what better distraction was there than a witchy challenge? I packed up my things, gave Mr. Charming a peck on the beak, and hugged Bessie. Then I nudged Cooper from his curled-up position in the window, where he'd gone for a quick nap the second the power went out.

"What? Can't a cat get a nap anymore?"

"You literally sleep eighteen hours a day."

"I need my beauty sleep if I want to keep up my dashing good looks."

"For what? You haven't been on a kitty date like ever, and in case you forgot, you can't make babies."

"No, but I'd have fun trying."

Bessie giggled. "He must be from the sixties. It was the time of free love and all that."

I held out my palm. "Please."

She threw back her head and laughed.

Cooper stretched his body into a downward kitty and then a reverse downward kitty and groaned. "A guy's got to do what a guy's got to do."

I shook my head. "Of all the familiars in the world, I had to end up with the snarky one. Come on, we're going on a field trip."

"What?"

"We're going to see Holiday Hills from a human view."

"I pretended to be a boring old cat for years. Why would I want to step back into that world?"

"Because duty calls."

"Well, my receiver is off the hook."

"You really must be from the sixties."

"A familiar never tells."

"Whatever. This is important. There might be a flux in the system, and I want to see if I can find it."

"You realize that's a bunch of crap, right? There's no such thing as a flux in the system."

"Then let's go prove Mr. Hastings wrong." I made the *come-on* motion with my hand. "Let's go."

"You're so getting me a can of salmon for this."

It was dark as midnight outside. If not for the solar-powered streetlights, it would be hard to tell it wasn't the middle of the night.

"This isn't a power surge or outage. Look at how dark it is out here."

"Weather happens," my familiar said.

"Weather is one thing. This isn't weather. There's no sun. Literally, it's like the sun has disappeared."

"It's the middle of winter. Half the world doesn't see the sun in winter."

"That's an exaggeration."

"My point is this isn't some magical—what'd you call it?"

"Flux, and I didn't create the phrase. Mr. Hastings did."

"Fine. Magical flux. It's just winter weather. Rain and clouds and—" He stared up. "I can admit, an unusually dark sky, but nothing we've never seen before."

"I've never seen it before."

"It's annoying working with a newbie sometimes."

"Rude."

He was mostly right. We didn't get bountiful amounts of sunshine in February, but still, this was Georgia, not Alaska, and we did actually see the sun during the winter months. "There's not even little rays peeping through the clouds."

"Because the clouds are thick. Trust me, I know what I'm talking about. This isn't some magical conundrum. It's just weather."

Several stores had generators, and soon their lights added a soft glow to the darkened day. Other stores used candles, and though they cast a similar glow inside, they did nothing to brighten outside.

I blinked, and when I opened my eyes, the day was completely normal. Rays of sunlight beamed down from between the clouds and warmed my cheeks with their touch. When I blinked again, it went back to night. "Whoa."

"What?"

Cooper pawed me just below my knee. I picked him up and cradled him like a baby. I'd done this before I knew I was a witch with a talking magical cat, and though it took a while to get back to such intimate things, it was happening more than before. If I thought about it too much, it was awkward, so I tried not to. "It's not dark in the magical world now. It's just a normal day."

"Okay, that's a little strange."

"Told you something was up."

"Wait," he said. "This doesn't make sense. It was dark at Bessie's, and everyone saw it."

"Maybe it started as some kind of power surge but something magical got a hold of it."

"To what? Mess with our heads?" he asked.

"You have a better theory?"

"Can't say that I do."

"Well, there you go."

A human crowd began to gather outside. They all stared at the sky in awe.

"Looks like our main power source is covered in clouds," someone said.

"What's going on?" another person asked.

A third said, "It's the apocalypse. I knew it was coming."

"It's not the apocalypse. That's not coming until after the aliens. This is the aliens."

Dear Goddess, I thought. The humans had gone all kinds of crazy, and I teetered right on the top of the sanity fence, leaning a heck of a lot closer to the crazy side than I'd like.

Bessie and the other magicals in the Enchanted experienced the darkness inside, but it only impacted humans outside. Why would that happen? I decided to play it cool. That's what Gabe would do if he were here. Which he should have been! "It's not the aliens," I said. "It's a power outage."

"Without the sun?" someone hollered.

The rain poured down on us. "People, it's cloudy and raining. Of course the sun is hidden. Calm down, please."

Gabe made his way through the crowd. He winked at me. "We've had an explosion at a power plant in Cumming. It's impacted Holiday Hills, Dahlonega, Dawsonville, and Cumming. I'm told it could be at least thirty-six hours before it's up and running again. In the meantime, everyone should calm down. Glenn Burns from ABC Weather says we're in for a few days of darkness and rain, which isn't uncommon this time of the year."

"Something feels different," someone said. "The darkness is really dark."

"That's crazy talk," another replied.

"Now, now." Gabe put his hands on his waist. "Don't be talking like that. This is simple math. North Georgia plus winter equals clouds and rain."

He made it sound like it was no big deal, and I hoped he was right.

"Now, go on, get your things in order, just make sure you don't buy up all the milk, bread, and eggs at the grocery. This isn't a snowstorm we're talking about. It's just a simple power outage on a stormy day."

Someone in the small crowd yelled, "And don't get all psycho about the darn toilet paper."

I had to laugh. Apparently making French toast during a power outage is a national thing. Everyone buys milk, bread, and eggs. They must never run out of syrup. Toilet paper was a new thing, and I had a feeling it would be the first thing to go. Humans were so predictable. I scooted up next to Gabe and whispered, "Can we talk?"

"Gimme a sec." He finished up with the crowd and pulled me aside as they dispersed. "What's going on?"

"It's a flux in the system."

He tilted his head and smiled. "Say that again?"

"That's what Mr. Hastings called it, but the more I think about it, the more I realize it's probably just an expression. It's when the magical and human worlds go off sync or something. We see things as they should be, but the human world has a different view. That's probably why it's freaking them out."

"I'm confused. What exactly is freaking them out?"

"See, that's just it. You don't see it because you're a magical."

"As are you."

"Yeah, but for whatever reason everyone at Bessie's saw it happen."

He sighed and ran his hand over his cropped hair. "Saw what happen?"

"The flux!"

He put his hands on my shoulders. "Honey, I adore you, but I don't have the slightest idea what you're talking about."

"I know you're going off what you think is happening, but it's more than that. It's so dark, and you can't even see the sun above the clouds."

"That's normal for this time of the year."

Why did the men in my life have to side with each other

all the time? "I know, but this feels different. It's really, really dark."

"And Mr. Hastings thinks that some kind of, what did you call it?"

"Flux. Do me a favor. Cast into human space. You'll see what I mean."

He closed his eyes, and when he opened them, his mouth dropped. "Holy cow. It's like the middle of the night."

"That's what I'm saying!"

"I wish I would have known this before I spoke to everyone."

"They seem to be less concerned since you did. I'm going to see if I can figure out what's going on."

"Promise me you won't put yourself in any danger," Gabe said. His eyes filled with something Stella assured me was love even though we'd yet to use those words. "I don't want anything to happen to you."

I shrugged that fear off with a, "Pfft. I'm a pro at danger."

"Abby, I'm serious."

I knew he was. Being a witch was hard enough, but being a witch with an overprotective magical boyfriend slash cop slash MBI operative was a lot of work. "I promise. Geez." And I meant it, only things never turn out the way I plan.

COOPER and I made our way through town, stopping at every store on Main Street, hoping we could get a grip on the severity of what was going on, and maybe even figure out the who and why. It was a long shot, but I felt pretty confident I'd learn something helpful.

Amber Ways, Ginger Amber's essential oils and candle

shop, a magical store on the far end of the street, was our first stop. It was one of my favorite stores for essential oils, but it wasn't the only place in Holiday Hills to offer them. Cassie's boutique had them, and so did Daisy Warbington's flower shop. The stores didn't compete as their oils were designed for specific and very different reasons.

People think the word ginger's relationship to redheads started in the new millennium, but Ginger was proof it started long before. She once told me she'd been named Ginger because of the color of her hair.

She was a nice witch who'd always given me freebies even though I could afford to pay. I learned a long time ago that not accepting a gift from a Southerner, even a witchy one, was poor manners, so I took them. I just left a little something in the tip jar to feel better about it.

She greeted me and Cooper like the world wasn't black beyond her door. Somewhere in her mid-fifties, she'd lived in Holiday Hills since long before I was born, and her Southern accent was as thick as they came. "Well, hey there, Abby Odell. I was just fixin' to make myself a spot of tea. Would you like some?"

"No, but thank you. I just wanted to come check on you and see if you're okay."

She set her tea kettle on the small electric pot heater on the back counter. "Why would you think I'm not?"

I explained why.

"Oh Goddess, that's not good, now is it? What does Miss Bessie say?"

"Bessie didn't realize either," I lied.

"Looks like we've got a playful witch on our hands, now don't we? Playful or downright devious."

"What do you mean?"

"I know you're new to the magical world, but don't sweat

this. Witches do this kind of thing all the time. We just love messing around with our human counterparts."

"That's cruel."

She shrugged. "It's better than a zombie apocalypse."

"Those aren't real."

She raised an eyebrow. "You sure about that?" She laughed. "See? I told you witches like to mess with people, and that includes other witches too."

I thought it through out loud. "They do like to play tricks on humans over Halloween."

"Oh, I have been known to play a Halloween trick on a human or two. It's hard not to during such a spooky season."

"If you had to guess, who do you think would be bold enough to play a joke of this size?"

She dragged her bottom teeth over her upper lip. "I'd say have yourself a little talk with Miss Newbie down yonder. Never can tell what that witch is up to, and I don't trust her one bit."

"Miss Newbie?"

She laughed. "Silly me, I have nicknames for everyone. Miss Mayflower, the owner of Vintage Mass." She leaned closer. "If you ask me, something wicked this way came, and it's moved in and put up shop."

Huh. Maybe there was a little competition between the stores after all? I wondered what Ginger Amber said about me behind my back. I chose to believe she thought I was awesome. "What makes you say that?"

"Oh, sugar, that witch is evil as they come. You know why she came here, right?"

"Can you remind me?"

"Because she practically got kicked out of Salem, that's why!" The tea kettle whistled, and she turned off the electric burner. "Now, you know I don't like talking ugly about our people, but my cousin Odessa Amber Quartermaine told me the town forced her out because she'd been caught targeting other witches. I can only imagine what she does to humans."

"But that's just a rumor."

"Honey, there's no such thing as rumors, especially when it comes to witches. During the trials, we all lived in fear because of rumors, but they weren't actual rumors, now were they?"

I blinked. "Did you just say during the witch trials?"

She smiled, then dug into the glass cabinet underneath the counter. "My Fountain of Youth Essential Oil. It's fabulous for the skin." She examined my face closely. "Might do you some good."

"Miss Ginger, let me make sure I've got this right. Are you saying you were in Salem in 1692 and '93?"

"Of course I was. I was seventeen when the trials started." She handed me the oil. "I'm here to tell you, this works."

Apparently so, I thought. She looked darn good for her age, and I was a bit taken aback by the fact that I was talking to a 345-year-old witch. "Oh, wow!" I didn't know what else to say to that. "Just, wow!"

I'd heard stories of witches from the 1600s being alive in my time, but I didn't think I'd ever meet one.

"I've got a special mix that can help you live a long and prosperous magical life also."

I held up my hand. "Thanks, but I'll go with the plan as it stands. I'm not sure I can handle 345 years of this."

She laughed.

I wanted to talk to her more about her time in Salem. I had so many questions. It was one thing to read a book, but to have a living, breathing person from such a tragic time in history to answer my questions was nothing short of miraculous. It would have to wait for another day, though. I had something more important to figure out first. "Are you saying Cassie Mayflower is responsible for doing something to the town magically? That she manipulated the power and sun to disappear from the sky?"

"Any witch can affect power. That's basic witchery 101. Witches can't affect Mother Nature, sweetie, and I hope you know that."

"I do, of course, but then how is this happening?"

"It's an optical illusion. She's created an illusion for humans, which is why magicals don't see it unless they try."

"Why would someone do that?"

"Because they think it's fun." She set a bottle of essential oil in a bag. "I'm not saying it's appropriate witch behavior, and I'd certainly never do anything like it myself, but some witches think it's okay."

"It's not."

"No, it isn't, but I'm afraid that's only part of it."

"What do you mean?"

"Sometimes magicals do things like this to target other witches to be blamed. That's exactly what happened with Cassie in Salem."

"She targeted another witch? That's horrible."

"It's not the way you think. She did something she shouldn't have done, and it was awful. Witches died because of her and some had to leave forever so they wouldn't be terminated. She should have been punished for her actions, but instead, she was sent away."

"What?"

She shrugged. "Witches were less apt to kill other witches back then. Things changed a hundred years later, but now we're back to a degree of civility. Unfortunately, it doesn't look like Cassie is interested in playing nice."

"So, you think she's playing with humans, and it's not a joke to her?"

"May I ask how you learned about the blackout?"

My stomach sank. "I saw it happen."

"Then whoever is doing this, Abby, is making sure you're involved. Perhaps they're out for you."

"What makes you think that?"

She pointed to her temple. "Witch's intuition."

"Okay, thank you," I said, and walked out before she could see the tears pour down my face.

Cooper had gone out on his own, slinking around town for clues, he'd said, but I had a feeling that was a lie. If I knew my familiar, he was hitting up his human friends for a can of fish.

I twisted my purse strap between my fingers. Ginger and Cassie were alive during the Salem witch trials. I'd never really seen them interact, which made perfect sense given what Ginger said, but were her comments just leftovers from a scorned old witch, or was Cassie a real threat? And why would Cassie play such a cruel joke on humans? Did a human upset her? I hadn't heard of anything, but that didn't mean it hadn't happened. Had she not cast the illusion properly? Was that why everyone at the Enchanted saw the store go dark? Or was it just a power outage, as Gabe had said?

The more I tried to figure it out, the more confusing it got. The only thing I could think to do was talk to others and see what they could tell me. I'd get to Cassie's shop, but first I wanted to have more information.

I continued my store-to-store examination, stopping next at Blooming Blossoms, Daisy Warbington's flower shop.

She'd opened the shop before I was born, and until recently, had always thrived.

"Hey, Miss Daisy, just wanted to come by and check on you. The darkness is overwhelming, isn't it?"

"It's dark?" She pushed her glasses up her nose. "I really need to fix my sight. Goddess knows it's a mess." She squinted through the small lenses. "Other than that, I'm doing well. I appreciate that you're checking on me."

Sweet Miss Daisy wasn't that old, but something about her gave off an old-person vibe, and I'd always felt like she needed a little extra attention. Witches aren't immune to illness, and they can't fix their ailments as easily as the stories say. We're meant to be a certain way, and no amount of magic can permanently fix us. Destiny always gets its way no matter how hard we try to change it.

I've known Daisy Warbington forever, and I believed I could trust her. "Have you heard about the darkness outside?"

She glanced out her window. "It's not dark?"

"Not for magicals, but it is for humans."

"Well now, isn't that strange?"

"Ginger Amber says witches like to play tricks on humans, and she thinks it's an illusion one of them created, except when it first happened, all of the magicals at the Enchanted saw it too."

"Oh, my goodness. Why would someone do that?"

"I can't think of any other reason it would be happening."

"Well, I have to agree with Ginger. Any number of witches or warlocks in town would do that. Magicals love to push human buttons, and sometimes they lump innocent magicals into their game. I'm sure it's all in good fun, though."

"If this was the only thing that happened, I'd agree, but humans are seeing magic too, and that's very concerning to me."

"How many humans?"

"Just one that I know of, but I haven't gone around town asking them if they've seen anything funny."

She smiled. "That's a good decision." Then she asked, "How do you know someone saw magic?"

"Because it was my best friend."

Her eyes widened. "Oh dear, that's not good. What happened?"

"She saw the broom at Cassie's sweeping all by itself."

"And what did you do?"

"Bessie and I, and then Cassie when she came in, convinced her it was a leftover Halloween prank."

"In February?"

I shrugged. "It was all we could think of at the time."

"As long as it worked, that's what matters."

I scanned the small store and noticed a few of the refrigerators were dark. "Are your coolers broken?"

"Unfortunately, that power surge must have blown a fuse or something. I tried to get it working, but my magic is a little rough around the edges these days."

"Would you like me to take a look?"

"That would be lovely, though I'm not sure it's going to make a difference." The happiness in her eyes disappeared.

"What do you mean?" I asked.

"I may have to close the store. I'm not selling like I used to, and I'm struggling to stay afloat."

"Oh, no. I'm sorry."

"I am too. I've worked so hard to build this business, but people just aren't buying flowers anymore. They're growing their own, and I can't compete with magical or human gardens."

"Surely you have human customers who don't have gardens. I know I've bought many flowers from you."

"Things are changing, Abby, and I don't think Blooming Blossoms is going to make it."

"Not if I can help it," I said. "Where's that fuse box?"

She led me into the back of the store, and I piddled with the stuff like I knew what I was doing, which I absolutely did not. After a few seconds of blindly messing with things I wasn't sure could electrocute me, I just waved my hand and magically fixed it for her. "There you go!"

She hugged me. "Oh, thank you so much!"

"Now's the perfect time to sell flowers. Tell everyone they'll brighten up the darkness. I'm sure it'll work."

"I think you might be right!"

When I walked back outside, the power, which had been flickering on and off over the past hour, was restored. I breathed a sigh of relief. That was a good indication that it really was a power surge and not part of a cruel magic trick. I blinked, and when I opened my eyes, the darkness had disappeared in the human sphere. Happiness rushed through me. Whoever caused the illusion stopped the game, and all would return to normal.

I headed back to the Enchanted. By the time I arrived, as I thought about everything that had happened so far, I'd gone from thinking it was over to heck no, someone did this on purpose.

And I was determined to find out who.

3

I told Bessie everything I'd learned. It wasn't much, but at least it made a little sense.

"Let me get this straight." She leaned against the counter with a cup of tea while Mr. Charming perched on her shoulder. "The power went back on and then the sun appeared."

"Yes, ma'am."

"I think Ginger's right about it being an illusion. Mother Nature is powerful, and magic simply can't manipulate it."

"Unless it's a rain spell or rain dance."

"Ah, but that's different." She walked behind the counter and contemplated a chocolate chip cookie by reaching her hand into the plastic case on top of the counter and then quickly removing it. "I don't need the calories."

I smiled. "Need and want are two entirely different things."

"Which brings me back to the rain thing. Rain is good for the environment."

"Most of the time."

She nodded. "I'll give you that. My point is, when natives

dance for rain, they do so because they need it. When magicals ask for rain, it's usually because they need it too. It's not manipulation when it's a need. It's a request."

I stared at the ground, thinking about what she said. "That makes sense. So, you think it was just lucky timing they both happened at the same time?"

"No, of course not. I think the sky lighting up at night was a precursor or a practice run for whoever decided to create the illusion."

"And what? Allowed me to see it?"

"That part stumps me."

"It all stumps me."

"It shouldn't. When the power flickered for those few hours, that was because of the storm. Whoever created the illusion must have waited for it to go back on and then dropped the illusion so it all coordinated."

"But why? What would be the point?"

Cooper strolled in with a gift neither Bessie nor I thought the Health Department would appreciate.

"Cooper Odell, get that thing out of here."

He dropped the chipmunk on the floor. It sat stunned for a second and then scurried out the door. I eyed Bessie.

She shrugged. "At least he didn't kill it."

"What she said," Cooper added.

I closed my eyes and shook my head. Sometimes arguing wasn't worth it. "Did you hear anything?"

"Nothing you probably don't already know. "The humans weren't as concerned as you were once their commander spoke."

"Commander?"

"Your boy toy."

Bessie chuckled.

"He's not my boy toy. He's the chief of police."

"And significantly older than her, so he's definitely not a boy," Bessie said.

I glared at her.

"Well, it's the truth."

"We all know my...Gabe is older than me. It doesn't need to be brought up every time we discuss him."

The two looked at each other, then shifted their eyes to mine.

Bessie spoke first. "I don't think we've really brought it up at all."

"We haven't," Cooper said. "She's just touchy about it because he's robbing the cradle."

I groaned. "Whatever. Can we please get back to the humans and the events of the morning?"

"Like I said, they listened to the chief and their favorite weather dude, and once the power went back on for good and the sun came out, they were copesetic." He stretched and rolled over to lick his stomach. "It's like they've already forgotten."

"I haven't," I said.

He groaned. "Of course not."

"I'm sorry, but I think something fishy is happening, and I want to make sure it doesn't happen again."

"You can't prevent something you don't know is going to happen," Bessie said.

"I know, but you're forgetting something very important in all of this."

"What?"

"The sweeping broom? Cassie obviously didn't do it, but someone did. And the light display last night? Was that for me?"

"I saw it too," she said.

"That's my point. You saw the lights. Stella saw the broom. What's the link?"

Cooper chimed in. "Me."

I exhaled. "Or me."

"I'm not sure what you're getting at," Bessie said. She added more water to her teapot and set it on the small electric burner. "Because it's just one of those things. It happened, but it's not a big deal. I know you're a powerful witch, but that doesn't mean everything that happens is because of or to you."

"You make me sound like I think everything is about me, and I don't. I just think it's strange, and I'd like to at least look into it. If that's selfish, so be it."

Three teenage girls wandered inside. Their large backpacks were stuffed to the hilt with books, and they walked with a slouch. Back doctors would make a killing in the coming years. I smirked at the variety of hair colors. All surprisingly basic—brown, blonde, and red.

Bessie greeted them with a smile. "Hey, girls, what can I get you today?"

"Mr. Charming loves you," the parrot said.

The girls laughed. Except the redhead, who only smiled. She was too busy scanning the room for what I assumed was Atlas.

"Does he say anything else?" one of them asked.

"Mr. Charming, tell these young ladies how beautiful they are."

"Mr. Charming loves himself some pretty women."

They broke out laughing.

"They would have been impressed with my chipmunk-hunting skills," Cooper whispered.

As if.

The redhead glanced down at Cooper. Had she heard

him? If so, she was a magical, but she didn't strike me as the kind.

The clock struck four o'clock, its chime echoing in the café.

"Is Atlas here?" the redhead asked.

I was right. She was looking for him.

Bessie glanced at the clock. "I'm afraid he's running late today." Worry flashed on her face. "I hope he didn't get in trouble for being late to class this morning."

"I'm sure he's fine," I said. "Probably in detention." I looked at the blonde girl. "Is that still a thing?"

"Detention? Uh, yeah, but only the strange kids get it. The cool ones, like Atlas, always seem to get out of it."

As if on cue, Atlas charged through the Enchanted's front door with a heavy sigh. "Sorry I'm late," he said, rushing into the kitchen.

Bessie and I stared at each other as the girls giggled amongst themselves.

Cooper hopped onto the counter and pushed his way into my arms. "That kid has nothing on me. I could charm these chicks with a flick of my tail and a rub against their legs. They'd be putty in my paw."

The redhead smiled. When she caught me watching her, she dropped her head so I couldn't see.

"I'll be right back," Bessie said, and followed Atlas into the kitchen.

"That boy is *fine*," the brunette said.

"He's so perfect," the blonde said. "Did you see how he smiled at me?"

I must have missed that, I thought.

"He didn't smile at you! He winked at me."

I twirled my wrist, and the girls froze.

"Channeling your inner Piper Halliwell?" Cooper asked. He loved the show *Charmed*, and Piper was his favorite character. Not only did he think she was the prettiest of the girls, he said she reminded him of someone he used to know. When I asked who, he brushed me off and changed the subject.

"I didn't want them to get out of hand."

"Out of hand? Really? They were too busy drooling over him." His entire body trembled, and I knew he was getting annoyed. "Don't know why. He's not the ten I was back in the day."

My eyes widened.

"Oh, my bad. We're not allowed to talk about that. I forgot."

Cooper liked to throw out hints about his past, his true self, but he was right. Familiars aren't supposed to share their pasts with their chosen ones. I had a feeling most of what he said wasn't true anyway. Cooper liked to get me riled up, knowing I could push the issue for hours and get nowhere. Cats had a lot of patience, but I learned to either ignore him or throw back a joke.

"I didn't know familiars could remember prehistoric times."

He hissed at me and bolted from my grip to sit under the table and sulk.

"Oh, is he mean?" Blondie asked.

I hadn't realized the freeze wore off so quickly. Maybe they were all witches? I could freeze humans until I chose to unfreeze them, but witches could usually push through the spell on their own. "No, he's just mad because I won't give him any tuna."

She stared at the brunette. "Weren't we talking about Atlas?"

Just then he walked from the kitchen. "Again with the perfect timing," I said.

"What?" he asked.

I winked at him. "I'll fill you in later."

The girls gathered around the table next to mine, each pulling out a chair and angling it toward the counter where Atlas worked. The redhead hadn't said much, and each time Atlas glanced their way, she quickly stared at the tabletop.

"Interesting," I mumbled under my breath.

Cooper climbed onto my table. "What's interesting?"

"Do me a favor, whisper. I think they're witches, and for whatever reason, they don't want us to know."

"Really?"

I nodded. "Definitely the redhead. She looked at you every time you said something."

"Maybe she's got the hots for me?"

"Yes, that's it."

"Kitty love's a thing. Check the internet."

"Please stop."

He meowed, but it sounded like he said *oh-la-la*.

I flicked my head toward the back of the café where Bessie still kept the shelves of new and gently used books. I walked over and stepped behind the third one. "Red won't look Atlas in the eyes, and she's been super quiet around him."

"Some guys have that effect on a woman."

It was going to be an eye-rolling week, for sure. "Seriously."

"Maybe she's just shy?"

"Or maybe she's hiding something?"

"Everyone's hiding something."

"True, but she's a child."

"She's what, sixteen? In cat years, that's dead."

I cringed. "You have an awful sense of humor."

"And you have a strange aversion to gifts."

"I do not," I said, crossing my arms over my chest.

"Chipmunk."

I closed my eyes and shook my head. "That wasn't a gift. It was prey."

"You don't understand cats, do you?"

"Of course I do. It's just gross when one tries to give me a helpless rodent as a gift."

He stood on his hind legs and shrugged. "To each his own."

I rolled my eyes. "Focus, please. My point is she won't look him in the eye, and she's hiding that she's a witch."

"You don't think this is about you too, do you?"

I narrowed my eyes. "Maybe she likes him and she's doing it to try and impress him."

"Babe, listen. I love ya. I do. I'm not sure we'd be a thing if I wasn't, you know, walking on four legs and all, but I love ya, so I've got to be honest here, okay?"

I tilted my head and sighed. "What?"

"That's the stupidest thing I've ever heard."

He was probably right, but I was pulling at straws to figure out who could be so cruel to humans, and why they'd involve me. "But it's possible."

"How exactly is that?"

"Because Atlas kind of has a crush on Stella, and Stella's my best friend, and maybe this young witch knows. You know how spiteful teenage girls can be. Teenage witches have to be a thousand times worse."

"You have no idea."

"See! That's my point. It's possible."

"About as possible as the world being flat." He meowed to soften the blows he repeatedly threw at my ego. "I'm not saying this isn't about you, but I doubt a teenage witch would have the ability to do all that. They're more likely to throw pies in people's faces, that kind of thing."

"If it turns out I'm right—"

"I'll acknowledge it."

"That's all I'm asking," I said.

When we returned to the café section of the store, the redhead was gone.

"Where's your friend?" I asked, using my most casual, innocent voice.

"Emma? She left," the blonde said. "She said the vibe in here was too negative for her."

I raised an eyebrow.

"She's retro like that. Thinks she's some throwback hippie or something."

Bessie walked out of the kitchen with a plate of chocolate chip cookies and placed it in the middle of the girls' table. "Here's a special treat from Atlas." She glanced at me and winked.

"Is it?" the brunette asked.

"I guess you'll have to ask him to find out!" She smiled and walked away from the girls.

I pulled Bessie to the side. "Hey, I know you're not a fan of Cassie Mayflower."

She straightened a stack of flyers someone from the library dropped off the day before. "What do you mean?"

"I didn't get to tell you what Ginger said about her."

"Honey, you live in a small town in the South. Everyone has something to say about everyone."

"I know, but this is kind of big." I chided myself for not mentioning it before, but I wanted to sit on it and see if I could get anywhere with it on my own before gossiping. "So, am I right?"

"Let's just say I've heard the rumors."

"And you believe them?"

"What did Ginger say?"

"She said she and Cassie were alive during the Salem witch trials."

She nodded.

"You knew?"

"I might have heard that."

"Wow. Oh, and she said Cassie was basically kicked out for causing trouble for other witches." I pressed my lips together.

"Basically kicked out and kicked out are two entirely different things, Abby."

"The point is, she was wreaking havoc and doing things to witches. Kind of like what's happening here."

"I wouldn't say that's exactly what's happening here."

"Again, how do you explain seeing that light display in the middle of the night?"

"You think Cassie did it?"

"It definitely falls under the screwing-with-other-witches column."

"Your mother wouldn't take kindly to you spreading ugly things about fellow witches."

I stuck out my bottom lip. "I'm not spreading ugly things. I'm discussing them with a confidante."

"You say dinner, I say supper, but we're both talking about the same thing."

"Fine. There is a rumor that Cassie Mayflower was targeting witches in Salem."

"And?"

"And the broom was sweeping outside her store."

"That could be a simple hiccup in the magical world."

"On the same day the lights all burst into life for us to

see? Only us? And the same day the power surged and the sun disappeared but only for humans? Sounds fishy to me."

She organized the already-in-order teabags in the tray on the counter. "I think you're making too much of this. Think about it. If Cassie was kicked out of or asked to leave Salem, that's a pretty big deal. Do you think she'd take the risk of doing something to cause that to happen somewhere else?"

"For all we know, she could have been kicked out of the last place she lived, and that's why she's here."

"Or perhaps she just wanted to live somewhere warmer? Massachusetts gets awfully cold this time of year."

"The broom, Bessie. Come on. If you give me nothing else, you can't say that's not strange."

"Possible magical hiccup aside, I'll admit that one's a little iffy." She closed the lid on the coffeemaker after adding fresh water. "But I don't think it's as dark and devious as you make it sound."

"I'm not so sure."

"What's the expression your momma always used to say?"

"Which one? She had hundreds."

She smiled. "You're making a mountain out of a mole hill."

I inhaled, then exhaled slowly. "That's the one I disagree with right now."

"Of course you do, dear."

GABE COULDN'T MAKE it that night after all, but Stella was up for a little pizza and a good romance movie.

She dropped onto the couch and kicked up her legs,

securing her feet on my coffee table. "What a day! I'm seriously going to look for another job."

I paid the Domino's delivery guy and sent him off with a smile.

"What's the awful smell?" she asked.

"I got Coop some anchovies. No seasonings, and on the side."

My familiar was already on my small dining room table waiting patiently for his gourmet meal. As I prepared it, juggling it with one hand while holding my nose with the other, Stella filled me in on why she wanted to quit editing books.

"And then she actually had the nerve to say my editing style is too harsh for her inner child. Can you believe that?"

Kind of? "You can be a bit harsh at times." I coughed while saying, "Word vomit."

"Oh, geez. Are we going there again?"

"I'm kidding."

"Good, so you know what I told her, right?"

"That you'd try to be more sensitive?"

"LOL, you're funny. I told her she should go back to kindergarten with that inner child and learn how to structure a dang story!"

"My bestie, winning friends all over Zoom."

She groaned. "Maybe I should be an attorney?"

"You'd be a killer prosecutor."

"I hear law school is super expensive."

My lights flickered. I quickly flicked my hand and made sure they stayed on. Thankfully, Stella was too involved in thoughts of law school to notice. I set Cooper's delicacy on the floor and offered it to him with a bow. I would have left it on the table, but I couldn't stand looking at the stuff. "Your dinner, Your Highness."

"As it should be," he said, and climbed down the table leg. He snarfed the fish down in a few quick bites, burped, then retreated to the window to watch the world pass by.

"Word vomit incident aside, tell me the truth. Do you think I'm too harsh?"

I handed Stella a plate with two slices of green pepper, mushroom, sausage, and black olive pizza. "Not at all."

"I feel like you're lying."

I sat beside her and smiled. "Not at all."

She eyed me suspiciously. "Liar. I know your lying face."

"Okay, maybe a little. But it's a white lie."

She laughed. "Great. Now I feel bad."

"Don't. She probably needed to hear it anyway. How about you practice on me?"

"Do tell."

"I'm struggling with my story, so how about I tell you, and you tell me what you think?"

"Even after word vomit?" She took a bite of her pizza slice.

"If you can channel your inner sensitivity for me, you can channel it for anyone."

"Fine, I'll give it a shot."

"Okay, so Adelle's town is filled with witches and humans, and something strange is happening. Usually the humans can't see magic, but now they can."

"And?"

"And one of the witches in town was basically kicked out of her hometown for targeting other witches."

"So, a simple storyline with one suspect? Really? You're better than that."

"Whoa. You are harsh. I'm not done yet."

She shoved the bottom portion of her pizza slice into her

mouth and, while chewing, said, "I'll just wait to comment, then."

I gave her a replay of what wasn't at all my current work in progress but instead a lighter version of my real-life situation. Minus a whole lot of truth. I only did it to gauge her level of "what if" in the possibility of magic. Three days ago I would have said she didn't believe, but the broom sweeping threw her for a loop.

"It sounds like a fairly simple story."

"But does it sound believable? You know I always want an element of truth to my stories."

"This is a paranormal mystery. It's impossible to have an element of truth in that regard, but your characters have personalities, even the magical ones, and that adds an element of reality to it." She pressed her lips together and raised her eyebrows. "Though you could add some random person walking by a store and freaking out because they saw a broom doing the sweep dance. That might bring in more reality." She shivered. "I'm still totally freaked out by that."

"You know, there's no proof magic isn't real."

She laughed. "And there's no proof it is."

"So, you don't think some magical force was causing the broom to sweep?"

"I mean, yeah, it wigged me out. I'll give you that, but honestly, if magic was more than magicians playing mind games with their audience, wouldn't I have seen something long before now?"

Phew! Stella wasn't worried about magic, so at least I could cross one problem off my list.

"I think your story has a good foundation. Adelle needs to figure out who's trying to show magic to her town, but where I feel it's lacking, at least based on what you've told me, is you really don't have a strong list of suspects to choose from. How are you planning to meld them into the mix?"

"They're already there, they just aren't obvious."

"Okay, that's perfect. So, what's the problem?"

"I need a reason. Why would someone with the gift of magic want to ruin it for everyone else by exposing it to the world?"

She smiled. "Honey, you're an excellent story crafter; stop stressing about this. You know there are only a few reasons people do anything."

"Love, power, revenge, and money."

She nodded. "Which will be your reason?"

"I guess once I figure out who the bad guy is, I'll figure that part out."

"Didn't you outline?"

"Things aren't going as smoothly as I'd hoped."

"Tell me your possible motives by suspect."

I laid out what I knew, which added up to absolutely nothing. She leaned back into the corner of the couch and groaned. "You just need to rework your outline. Build a strong case against a few people, then flip it with a logical but not quite surprising ending. You know how to do this."

The problem was, I didn't really have any suspects. The best I could come up with was a transplant from Salem with a rumor of nastiness attached to her and absolutely no credible motive.

WE DROPPED the mystery subject and discussed other girly things, like the date she'd had with a guy she met at an editing event in Atlanta a few weeks ago. She'd gone between liking him, not liking him, and thinking he might be the one at least three times in our hour-long conversation.

"You've changed your mind about him three times since you brought him up. Every time you do this, it's because you want to like the guy, but you don't. Why even bother going out with him again?"

"Because what if I'm wrong? What if he is the one for me, and I'm just not in the right frame of mind to realize it?"

"Then he's not the one for you."

"But what if he is?"

"What if you stopped worrying so much about men and focused on you?"

She stuck out her bottom lip. "Harsh."

"No, it's not. And obviously, I don't mean there are things to focus on. I think you're perfect. My point is, you spend so much energy worrying about your happily ever after, you forget about the here and now."

"You can say that because you've found your happily ever after."

I didn't want to smile, but my mouth betrayed me. "We don't know that. Gabe and I barely know each other."

"Doesn't mean it's not fate."

"Fate is yet to be seen."

After she left, I decided to write out everything I knew and see where that led me. When I outline a novel, I usually list the murder—which there wasn't in this case—the victim, and then each suspect with a motive, alibi, and lie. Once I have those figured out, I can summarize each chapter and blend them into something at least a few readers will enjoy. If I'm lucky, the story will follow that outline. I'm not usually that lucky.

Unfortunately, my list was slim. Cassie Mayflower. Semi-snooty transplant rumored to have been kicked out of Salem for causing trouble. Motive? Nada. Alibi? Ditto, because technically, a witch can be in one location and create another situation miles away. Alibis in paranormal mysteries can be tough, and mysteries or crimes in real life can't have an alibi without a motive.

Or can they?

Since I had no other stand-out suspects—not that Cassie Mayflower exactly stood out—I had to include everyone I could think of who might be involved.

Again, the list was slim, but not as slim as the potential suspect list. I labeled it the "improbable suspect list" and added Mr. Calloway, Atlas Spencer, and the redhead high school girl I was pretty sure was a witch and acted all kinds of shady earlier.

Poor Mr. Calloway. As uncomfortable as he made me at times, he didn't appear to have a motive, and as a shifter, he wasn't privy to the magical elements of a witch or warlock. Yet, I wouldn't take him off the slim-pickings list. The bigger the list, the better the chance of finding the criminal. If he was involved, he'd need a partner, so I added the other two regulars as sub-improbable suspects in parentheses next to his name. They were a long shot, but in the magical world, long shots should always be considered.

Atlas Spencer. Could a young, popular warlock want to harm his community? Why? Maybe his principal punished him for being late? I tapped my pencil on the paper. "Doubt-ful," I said to Cooper, who lay snuggled in a ball next to me.

"What?" he asked.

"Atlas Spencer. What reason would he have to want to expose magic?"

He stretched out his front legs and stuck his little behind in the air, groaning out an annoyed meow in the process. "I still don't get why you think someone's trying to expose magic. A sweeping broom and a dark sky aren't big tricks that say doom and destruction for all magicals. They say someone's being a pain in the butt."

"You really think this is nothing?"

He hopped over to the small coffee table and sat on my papers. "People see magic all the time. It happens. Shifts in the Universe or maybe someone has a slight sixth sense, or whatever, but they see it all the time."

"I never did."

"Do you remember when you saw the sparkles of light around the Christmas tree at Adelle's?"

"You mean when I was five?"

He nodded.

"It was glitter. My mother said she'd tossed it onto the tree." I pressed my lips together when I realized where this was going.

Cooper laughed. "And there it is, the face of recognition."

"Wait, how do you know this? You weren't around when I was five."

"You keep thinking that."

I hate when he's snarky and doesn't answer my questions.

"My point is magic slips through the cracks of the Universe all the time." He held up his paw, examined it, then gave it a cleaning. It was his way of telling me I'm an idiot.

"Something just doesn't feel right."

"The flux in the system?"

I smiled. "I really don't think that's a thing."

"Yet you think this is a magical situation?"

"I don't see how you can't."

He shook his head. "I have a sense of things. I'm here to protect you, and with that comes a seventh sense of sorts."

He switched feet, and after examining the second one, decided it was clean enough. "Along with my unlimited number of lives."

I sighed.

"Do me a favor, step out of the magical place you live in and view it as a human place. I think you're off the mark here, that's all I'm saying. Worry about something else, or hey, how about you just enjoy life for a change? You're so wound up all the time. Maybe you should give my catnip a little sniff?"

"Yes, that's what I'll do."

He laughed. "Dude, it's awesome."

I got up and went to bed, the lingering sense of doom still hanging over me like a dismal rain cloud.

4

The sky lit up the night as bright as a Christmas tree. I opened one eye, noticing my bedroom looked like it did during the middle of the afternoon with the blinds up. Had I slept until afternoon? No way. That would be crazy, and Bessie surely would have checked on me. I glanced at my clock, then bolted out of bed and stared out the window. "Cooper, look! Don't tell me this is nothing. The sun is shining!" I glanced at my clock. "And it's not even three-thirty in the morning!"

He peeked out of a small opening in the covers and looked toward the window with one barely-open eye. "Did we sleep that late?"

"Look at the clock."

"Cats can't tell time."

I wasn't in the mood for jokes. "Cooper!"

He hissed, but he climbed out from the covers and perched on my windowsill. "Yeah, that's a little strange. You sure you didn't slip some of the nip into my milk before bed?"

"Yes, in fact, I did, and I added it to my water beforehand too. Come on, cat! You see my point now?"

He nodded. "I'll give you that it's a little strange, but we don't know if anyone else sees it."

The sun dimmed slowly until it darkened the night sky back to where it belonged. I kept an eye outside, watching the apartments on the second floors of the town's buildings for signs of life. Either everyone had blackout curtains or that display was only for me and Cooper.

Which made the whole thing even weirder.

"Go back to sleep. I'll be waking you up extra early for some tuna. And I'm going to want the whole can this time." He nuzzled back under the covers on his side of the bed.

I followed suit, but while Cooper's soft snores began seconds later, sweet slumber eluded me.

STELLA BARGED INTO THE ENCHANTED, tossed her bag on my regular table, and plopped into the chair across from me. She'd tossed her gorgeous hair into a bun, and was dressed in yoga pants, an oversized University of Georgia sweatshirt, and a pair of hiking boots. Stella was a fashionista, and even though she would be stunning in sweaty workout clothes, it wasn't normal for her, and I knew something was up.

"What the heck happened to you?" I played it cool, but mentally I was panicked.

"Okay, call me crazy, but weird stuff is happening to me."

I held my breath as she continued.

"Last night I got up to go to the bathroom and the sun was out."

I won't repeat the word that first came to mind. "Um..." I hated playing it off as nothing, but I didn't want Stella to freak, so what other option was there? "I'm sure you were dreaming."

"It didn't feel like a dream."

I leaned back in my chair all casual and chill like nothing ever bothered me. "Those are the best kinds of dreams, the ones where it feels real. The ones where you're running around town in your underwear are a little strange."

That seemed to settle her. Well, that and the magical calming essence Bessie had very likely sprinkled into her coffee, which she was guzzling down while I spoke. "It felt so real. I swear, I was up and out of bed."

"Sleep dreaming?" Bessie asked. "The other night I woke up in the family room trying to turn on my TV without the remote." She glanced at me and winked. "I can't remember the last time I had a TV without a remote. Maybe the 80s?"

"I would have liked to see that on video," I said. I loved that woman for helping me out.

Did that mean she saw the sun too? I'd have to ask her without Stella knowing. "Bessie, do you still have that book about the Salem witch trials?"

"Last row on the left, second shelf from the bottom."

"Would you mind showing me?"

"Of course," she said.

Mr. Charming hopped onto the back of my chair and stared at Stella. For reasons none of us really understood, the bird wasn't a big fan of my bestie, and she knew it. "Don't mind me. I'll just sit here while Mr. Not-So-Charming prepares to eat me."

"Mr. Charming is a good boy," he said.

"Whatever." She ducked as the parrot flapped his large green wings.

"He prefers fruit and nuts," Bessie said.

"He probably thinks I'm a nutty fruitcake."

I couldn't help but laugh.

Bessie and I hurried to the back.

"Why didn't you tell me?" I asked.

"Tell you what?"

"Did you see it this morning too?"

"Are you saying she's telling the truth?"

I nodded. "But you didn't see it?"

She shook her head. "I saw the look on your face and thought I should help."

"I was trying to act like everything was fine."

"You've never been good at masking your emotions, which is why you never got the lead in the school plays."

"Gee, thanks." I grabbed the book and flipped through the pages, stopping at one with a drawing that caught my eye. "Whoa." I rotated the book and showed it to Bessie. "Look familiar?"

Her eyes widened. "That looks like a younger Daisy Warbington."

"So you see it too?"

"I didn't know she was in Salem," Bessie said.

"Because it was in the 1600s and pretty hard to believe, right?"

"That's on you, sugar, not her. There are many witches here from back then. They just don't talk about it."

I still couldn't wrap my head around the fact that we had witches in my hometown who were close to four hundred years old, though the not-talking-about-it part seemed logical. Who would want to relive that kind of horror? "Bessie, do you think she could be doing this?"

"Why would Daisy want to wreak havoc on this town?"

I sighed. "You're probably right. She's a sweet woman,

and I always feel like I need to, I don't know, almost take care of her. She seems fragile sometimes."

"I think you're dealing with a lot of coincidence and maybe a witch or warlock who likes to create optical illusions. Maybe you're privy to them because your powers were bound for so long."

Atlas appeared in the aisle. "Oh, I'm sorry to bug you, but Miss Bessie, we just got a lunch to-go order for ten sandwiches. I can whip it up if you'd like?" He smiled at me and nodded. "Hey, Miss Odell."

Gawd. That made me feel old. "Atlas, seriously, call me Abby."

"Yes, ma'am."

"Honey, you have to get going. I'll take care of the order."

"You sure? I can stay to help."

"No, I don't want you getting in trouble at school. Now scoot."

"Yes, ma'am," he said, then smiled at me as he rushed off.

"That boy has a big crush on you. You get all ages, don't you?"

I blinked. "What? He's got a thing for Stella. He barely speaks when she's around."

She laughed. "Honey, you might need to get your eyes checked. He does it around you, not Stella. You just notice it when Stella's here."

I narrowed my eyes. "Huh. I had no idea." I closed the book. "May I keep this for a while?"

"Of course."

Mr. Charming was standing on my laptop, which, thankfully, was closed, and giving poor Stella a death stare. Bessie and I both laughed as we walked back to the main area of the Enchanted.

"Why does this bird hate me so much?"

Mr. Charming flew to Bessie's extended arm. "He doesn't. He's like a grade school boy. He picks on you to show his affection."

"No. He hates me."

"Mr. Charming loves you," the green parrot said.

"I think he's talking to you," Stella said to me.

The door swung open and the three girls pranced in.

"Hey, is Atlas still here?" the brunette asked.

"You just missed him," Stella said.

"Oh." The blonde sighed dramatically.

"Would you like your mochas this morning?" Bessie asked.

"Yes, ma'am," the blonde and brunette said.

Bessie smiled at the quiet redhead. "What about you, sweetie?"

"No, thank you." Her eyes darted around the store.

What was she looking for? I set the Salem book on the table and placed a spiral notebook on top of it. I caught the girl glance at the Salem book and quickly turn away. That was interesting. Was she interested in history, or the fact that I was interested in it?

Stella got to babbling about the guy she wouldn't end up with again, but I kept my eye on the three girls. I watched their interaction, noting neither the blonde nor brunette appeared to care what went on around them, but the redhead seemed awkward and uncomfortable. Maybe she was the new friend in the trio, or maybe she was tired.

High school was tough, especially for girls, and the magical element had to make things even more complicated.

After the girls left, and Stella had used up a good portion of her words for the day, I got to work on my investigation, paging through the book I'd borrowed from Bessie.

"You didn't mention Salem was part of your next book," Stella said.

I closed the book. "I've made some changes to the outline," I lied.

"You want to discuss?"

"Nope. I think I've got it now."

"Good." She finished her coffee, then yawned and tossed her laptop into her bag. "I'm heading home."

I glanced up at her as she stood. "What? Why?"

"I'm exhausted. That dream seemed so real, and I feel like I didn't get enough sleep." She stared down at her clothing. "And seriously, I need a shower."

I plugged my nose. "I wasn't going to mention that, but..."

She laughed. "Text or call me later."

"Will do."

I went back to the book, examining each page carefully, scanning through the words for something that stood out and taking notes when it did.

"Bess, come look at this!" I took a photo of a paragraph discussing two witches named Daisy Warbington and Cassandra Mayflower.

Bessie read the paragraph. "Interesting." She pulled out Stella's chair and sat. "This is unexpected."

"They were friends until Daisy threw Cassie under the bus."

"Unfortunately, that happened a lot back then. From what I understand, some witches may have been saved from hanging by bringing other witches to be hanged."

"That's awful."

"It was."

"But if Cassie was hanged, how is she still here?"

She read farther down the page. "She wasn't hanged. It says here she was spared but had to leave town because of what she did."

I continued reading. "Daisy told the town Cassie was a witch. Why would she do that?" I couldn't imagine living in a world where your best friend would want to watch you burn on a stake. What could have happened to push Daisy, sweet, sweet Daisy, to that place? And could she be the one messing with things in town? To blame her former friend and drive her away?

"The interesting part of the history of the trials is most of the women who were hanged weren't even witches. They were lost souls with psychological disorders that were misunderstood back then. It's all just a terrible tragedy," Bessie said.

"I need to talk to Daisy."

Bessie patted my shoulder. "Sweetie, Daisy may not show it, but she's a powerful witch. If what the book says is true, tread carefully. You can't be sure she won't hurt you for figuring it out."

She might have been right. In the past Daisy had struggled with her magic, but she'd acted like it was nothing. Was that for my benefit? To throw me off her scent? To make her appear innocent when she wasn't? "Maybe I should start with Cassie, then?"

"I'm not sure she'll tell you much. I know she doesn't like to talk about those times."

A customer came in, and Bessie excused herself to attend to him. "Just do me a favor, please. Be careful. We don't know what Daisy is capable of."

I could say the same thing about Cassie, too. She'd been ousted from Salem, which was probably tragic but also a good thing, because it obviously saved her life. But why, and at what expense? Could Cassie have been building up resentment over these past several hundred years in order to avenge her former bestie for ruining her very long life?

If that was the case, I now had to walk on eggshells around two witches. I didn't want either of them thinking I was onto them. Goddess only knew what would happen, and I feared it would be directed at Stella.

The best way to attack someone is through the people they love, and Stella's humanity, though her greatest strength, was no match for witchcraft.

CASSIE'S boutique door opened just as I walked up, but it wasn't electronic. "Well, hey there, sunshine. You here for some of my essential oils? They'll do wonders for your skin."

"Uh, sure," I lied. "I thought I'd have a look around." I held my purse tight against my side. I had to assume Cassie was a very powerful witch, and if she was guilty of what was happening, she might rip the Salem book from my grip and send me flying.

Anything's possible in magic.

She handed me a small bottle with a little dropper on it. "Just a drop of this and that worn, leathery look will disappear."

I touched my face. I wasn't aware I had a worn, leathery look. "Oh, thanks."

She crossed her arms and eyed me suspiciously. "Now honey, are you going to ask me what it is you came here for or keep pretending you're here for essential oils?"

I blushed. "I'm sorry." I removed the book from my purse.

She eyed it. "Well, I had a feeling you'd come about this."

"You did? Why?"

"The broom incident yesterday."

"Did you do that?"

She shook her head. "I did not, and I promise you that. If I were to guess who played that little trick on your friend and very likely created the optical illusion, I'd say it was Daisy, and I think you're here to find out why, aren't you?"

"That must be awful, having to deal with someone who dislikes you so much."

"She doesn't dislike me. She hates me, but I will admit, in her eyes she thinks it's justified, though I never did what she claims." She filled me in on what happened, and how they let a man come between them. "It's the same old story. Like human females, witches let a male get between them. Seems so pointless now, really."

"Do you think you'll ever resolve it?"

She laughed. "Oh, Goddess, no! That broom was burned in 1692. You don't forgive someone for throwing you to the wolves."

She had a point.

"Has she done things to you in the past? I mean, other than during the trials?" What a sensitive subject. I had no idea how to address the horrors she must have experienced, so I tried not to ask directly.

"Other than throw me to the wolves, not much. I left Salem for a long time, and when I finally felt comfortable enough to return, she was already gone. There were others, though, who took her place in tormenting me. Since I've moved here, she's tried a spell or two to cause me trouble, but nothing I couldn't handle."

"And you're sure it's her?"

"Who else would it be?"

"So, just to make sure we're on the same page, you think Daisy is doing this and trying to make you look guilty?"

She nodded.

"But why me? Why Stella? I don't understand that part of it."

"When someone, a witch included, is miserable, they want everyone to be just as miserable as they are. Every magical in Holiday Hills sees the gift of friendship you share with Stella, and I'm sure it causes wonder for some, but for Daisy, I believe it makes her mad. She had that once, but she lost it, and she'll be damned if anyone else has it now."

Whoa. Talk about crazy. If Cassie was right, Daisy's level of hate surpassed anything I wrote about in my books. How was I supposed to deal with that?

Cassie poured herself a cup of tea. "Would you like some?"

"No, thank you. I appreciate you being honest with me, and I'm so sorry to make you talk about something so tragic."

"Yes, it was a tragic time, and horrible things happened. The saddest part of the trials was that only two witches were murdered. The rest were just mentally ill women. So much tragedy for misunderstood, innocent humans." She wiped a tear from her eye. "Honey, I think it's best you let this lie. If Daisy is doing this, she'll soon take it to the next level, and she's a very powerful witch. Your friend might be an innocent victim in this, and you don't want to make things worse for her. Either way, neither you nor Stella are her targets. I'm her target. Let me fight my own battle. Promise me you won't go to Daisy with this. Please."

I made that promise, but I wasn't sure I could keep it.

THE HIGH SCHOOL girls sat at the table closest to the counter. The lunch rush had just ended, so I assumed the county schools had a half day. Atlas rushed in and tossed his bookbag behind the counter, then headed into the kitchen as the girls ogled him from behind.

"Hey, Miss Abby," the blonde said.

If they'd ever told me their names, I'd totally forgotten. I didn't want to seem rude, so I licked my lips and magically asked them to tell me on their own.

Atlas appeared at the counter, and the blonde elbowed the brunette.

"Where's your friend today?" I asked.

The blonde's upper lip pushed into a snarl. "Emma's out, and that's just the way I like it."

Ouch.

The brunette nudged her. "Amber, it's not nice to speak ill of the dead."

I furrowed my brow.

"To us," she said. "She's dead to us."

"Deader than a skeleton," Amber said. "Britney's right. She's not our kind of people anymore."

Ah, how I love magic. "Britney's right, but that doesn't just apply to the dead." I smiled. "My mother used to say what goes around comes around, so be careful with what you put out into the Universe."

"My mom always says what's wicked this way comes," Amber said. "And watch your back."

"Interesting."

Atlas held up the teapot and coughed. "Uh, Miss Abby, your usual?"

"Actually, I'd love a glass of ice water with a lemon, if you don't mind."

"Sure thing," he said, and poured me a tall glass from a Brita pitcher.

As I carried my things to my table, Mr. Charming flew over and balanced his clawed feet on my head. "Ouch, Mr. Charming! What's with your obsession with scalp-digging these days?" I grabbed him by the torso and gently removed him and two claws full of hair from my head.

He plopped onto the table. "Mr. Charming is cranky. Mr. Charming is cranky."

"Considering half my hair is now on the table, Abby is cranky too."

He flew to the counter and stuck his butt toward me.

The girls laughed.

Atlas handed me the water and then checked on the girls. They smiled and flirted with him, but I didn't really pay that much attention. I was too busy going through the rest of the pages in the book and enlightening myself on something so incredible, it could change the trajectory of magic in Holiday Hills forever.

GABE RESTED his work boots on my lap as he stretched out on my couch. "Are you sure?"

Cooper plopped onto Gabe's groin area and stretched his head up to my boyfriend's mouth. He sniffed, then turned to me and said, "He had fish for lunch."

Gabe gently picked Cooper up and set him back on the side of the couch. "Sorry, buddy. I did."

"Did you go to Freddy's for lunch?" I asked.

Gabe glanced at my cat. "I'll bring leftovers next time. If there are any."

"He won't," Cooper said, and hissed at Gabe as he backed away and hid in my bedroom.

"He doesn't like me."

"He does. He doesn't like that you didn't save any fish for him."

"At least I know for next time. Anyway, do you really think that's happening?"

"I don't think. I know."

He sat up and set his feet firmly on my floor. "You think Daisy would risk the secret of magic to continue a hundreds-year-old war, and you think she'd use you and Stella to do it?"

I nodded. "It makes perfect sense."

"I'm not sure about that."

"That's because you don't understand jealous women. Daisy and Cassie were best friends, but that friendship was ruined because of a guy."

"And how exactly is she using your friendship with Stella in this?"

"Maybe she sees how strong our friendship is, and she hates it, so she just made us part of it. Like if a human and a magical see what's happening, we'll try to figure out who's doing it. Which is sort of what's happening."

"You think you have that kind of power?"

"What do you mean?"

"To affect someone, a witch in particular, like that. Do you think that's possible?"

"What else could it be?"

"I don't have an answer for you. I just know Daisy isn't very powerful, and she's never sent any red flags to the MBI."

"Cassie says she's very powerful."

"Cassie's a little biased. If you really think Daisy's doing this, talk to her. You're far more powerful than any witch around. There's nothing for you to fear here."

"Cassie told me to stay away from Daisy."

He rubbed his chin. "Maybe because she's the one avenging what happened in Salem? You said she was kicked out of town, that Daisy threw her to the wolves. It makes sense that she'd be the one causing trouble and claiming innocence."

I gave that some thought. "How would I find that out?"

"Like I said, just talk to Daisy." He winked. "Her magic's nothing compared to yours."

"I appreciate that, and your theory makes sense. I don't know why I let Cassie manipulate my thoughts about Daisy."

"You're a very young witch. Someday you'll realize how powerful your magic is."

That jab didn't hurt, but I didn't necessarily like it either. "Your birthday's coming up. You want a nice present or a bag of toads?"

"I rather like toads," he said, and kissed my forehead. "I don't see a problem with you talking to Daisy, but I honestly think if you just drop it all, it'll lose steam and pass. Manipulating optical illusions is a lot of work. Whoever's doing it can't continue it for long."

I hoped he was right, but the feeling in my gut told me he wasn't.

5

Stella and I planned to meet in Dahlonega the next afternoon. I needed the change of scenery and time to clear my head and decide if I was making something out of nothing. Maybe Gabe was right. Maybe this was an old flame burning between two witches, and it would reach the end of the wick if I just let things lie.

Dahlonega is one of my favorite places. It's the perfect quintessential small town with a downtown square filled with quaint shops and fabulous little restaurants. What I love best is that it doesn't need to pretend to be something it's not. It's a picture-perfect Hallmark movie town, which is probably why it was picked as a location. Of course, North Georgia isn't a winter wonderland, so they pretended it was Ohio, but people from here knew the truth, and we were thrilled to have one of our small towns on the big screen.

The Picnic Café is an excellent lunch spot that serves the best freshly baked bread. Every time I go there, I buy a loaf to bring home. I don't even need to put anything on it, it's just that good.

I arrived there early, getting a rare parking spot right in

front. A man with a long salt-and-pepper beard who was bundled in a jacket and scarf sat at a small outside table sipping his coffee. He greeted me with a slight nod and then quickly disappeared. I blinked. Wasn't expecting that.

I ordered toast and coffee and removed my notes, the Salem book, and my laptop from my bag. I stretched, wishing I could have slept even a few minutes longer. Cooper wasn't with me, and I didn't mind the break. I dropped him off at the Enchanted with the agreement that he'd show up if necessary. As if that were ever a question anyway. I had no doubt his familiar radar was aimed straight on me and hadn't budged since I left him.

Stella wasn't set to arrive until after noon, and it was only eight-fifteen, so I ordered breakfast. After buttering my toast, I dug into the book again, working through it even more closely this time. I considered a spell to dig out what I might need, but magic isn't as easy as books like people to believe. I might be a newbie to the fold, but I liken witchy magic to leprechaun magic. You can cast a spell, but the Universe often puts a spin on it. Fate and destiny always have a plan, and no amount of magic can change it. One time I cast a spell to have my makeup applied magically. I'm horrible at doing it myself, and it was a special night with Gabe, so I wanted to look extra glamorous. The Universe took my spell to mean I wanted to look like someone famous, and I got that. Looking like Ronald McDonald wasn't exactly my plan. Gabe got a good laugh out of it all, and I got a bad case of chin acne from all the foundation.

A chill ran up my spine. I turned around, but no one was there. I glanced out the window, and a spray of sparkles flitted across my view. Magic lives everywhere, but it's rarely hidden from those who can see it. That didn't sit well with me. Why would a magical choose to hide? I glanced at the young woman who'd served my toast. She was staring out the window, and when she caught me looking at her, she quickly looked away. Interesting.

"Can I get you anything else?" She smiled, but the smile faded as she noticed my book. "Is that about the Salem trials?" She twisted her hands together. "Those were awful."

I nodded. "They were." I closed the book.

"I'm sorry. It's not my business, but may I ask why a witch would be studying something so awful for magicals?"

I raised my brow.

She shrugged. "My sister was here, and you felt her. I saw you turn when she floated by."

"Got it. Does she do that often?" I asked.

"She likes to hide. She's done that as far back as I can remember. I guess she's never really grown out of it."

"Nothing wrong with staying young at heart."

"I guess," she said. "I think it's more of a self-protection thing. Anyway, can I get you anything else?"

"Actually, I'm going to be here a while, so if you'd be willing to keep the coffee coming, that would be great. If you need the table, though, I'm happy to move."

She glanced around the café. "I think it'll be fine. May I ask what you're working on?"

"Oh, I write paranormal mysteries, so I'm doing some research for a book," I lied.

"Must be a pretty heavy mystery to need to research the trials."

"It's a little more intense than my normal ones."

She smiled and walked back to get the coffee pot. I thought about what she said about her sister. It reminded me of a toddler playing hide-and-seek, but I didn't want to be judgmental.

The book educated me on the trials more than I'd ever

wanted, and I sent good vibes out to the Universe for those who struggled through the tragedy, praying they'd found peace. I thought about Daisy and Cassie and what they must have experienced back then. To let a boy get in the way of a friendship and have it end so tragically was awful, but to set your friend up for death because the boy liked her was just evil.

Evil.

Ah! And there it was, the missing piece I needed. In most cozy mysteries, the villain is the most innocent character in the book. What if this situation was exactly what I thought, but I was just looking at it from the wrong angle?

Cassie told me about Daisy right from the start, effectively throwing her former bestie under the bus. In this game of Clue, Daisy looks guilty, while Cassie appears angelic. But...what if the opposite was true? What if this was Cassie's chance to get back at Daisy?

What if I spent too much time in my characters' worlds and not reality? Not only did this all sound stupid, it sounded ridiculous too. Two extremely old witches with a tragic past, and one suddenly decides to avenge something done so long ago? Why now?

Maybe Gabe was right. Leave well enough alone and it'll run its course. He had experience in crimes of magic, so I should trust him. I stuffed everything back into my bag, paid my bill, and sent Stella a text letting her know I was in dire need of a mental health day and wouldn't be meeting her after all.

There was nothing going on. I'd built a whole devious mystery in my brain because that's what I do for a living. There was always a logical explanation, but I hadn't looked for it. I simply aimed my efforts at the worst possible explanation, allowing my brain to create something else entirely.

But seeing a February night sky light up like the beach on a hot summer day brought me pause. Stella and I both saw that. How could that be my creative brain at work? Learning I'm a witch was like a walk in the park compared to trying to figure out this stuff.

I stopped at the fudge shop and purchased a chunk of peanut butter chocolate. I unwrapped it the second I walked out of the store and took a healthy bite. It was glorious, and immediately sent signals to the happy spot in my brain. Chocolate never disappointed.

I stopped in a small boutique and admired the long knitted scarves in both fall and winter colors. Even though Georgia winters weren't too cold, many of us longed for a wintery chill, so we pretended they were possible, and sometimes, our dreams came true. We wore coats and scarves and mittens and topped them off with knit hats with pompoms on top. Then we sweated our butts off, but on those one or two days a year when a natural chill filled the air, it was worth it.

The chill ran up my spine again. I turned around, but no one was there. "You don't have to hide from me," I said, smiling.

The sparkles floated toward the park beside the square and then formed into someone I recognized. She bowed her head and walked up slowly, as if she was ashamed.

"Shouldn't you be in school?" I asked.

Emma, the redhead from the Enchanted, shrugged. "School's boring, and I don't really like anyone there anymore."

I felt for her. It was hard enough being a teenager, but the added element of the craft couldn't make it easier. All those hormones plus magic? That would be a lot to handle.

"I understand something happened with Britney and Amber. I'm sorry about that."

"They're losers," she said, kicking a small pile of gravel on the side of the road. "I don't need them. They're magicals, and I mean, yeah, that makes things more fun, but I don't need to waste my time with them if they're going to turn on me like they did."

I nodded. "You can share your life with humans too. My best friend isn't magical."

"My mom says that, but human girls are worse than magical ones. Besides, things are different than when you were my age."

I shook my head. "I'm pretty sure girls are still the same. Things you have might be different, but people, human or otherwise, don't seem to change." I sounded old and wise! My mother would be proud. "What happened with you guys?"

"They're mad because of Atlas."

Of course, a boy. Not at all shocking. Seems that had been going on for hundreds of years. Probably since the beginning of time. "Care to explain a little more?"

"Britney likes him, and she's, like, the leader of the group, I guess, so Amber and I are supposed to be, like, all hands off and stuff."

"Beings, human or otherwise, aren't property someone else owns, and feelings certainly aren't under our control. Not all the time anyway. Did you tell Britney or Amber you like him? Is that what this is about?"

She shook her head. "He asked me to the winter formal."

Ouch. That had to sting. Those girls seemed pretty aggressive in their pursuit of all things Atlas. "That's exciting!" It was exciting even though it came with a ton of negatives for the young girl.

"I said no."

"You did? So you're not interested in him?"

She shrugged. "I mean, I think he's a total ten and all, but they're telling everyone I'm now the biggest, you know..." She left the word unsaid. "And I don't want people thinking that about me."

"Listen, this stuff happens, but it's kind of like the gossip rags you see at the grocery store. One celeb is attacked, and two days later, it's totally forgotten because people have already moved on to the next biggest piece of gossip. Give it a few days and it'll go away."

"You obviously didn't have the internet when you were my age."

"How old do you think I am?"

She shrugged. She did that a lot. "Maybe forty?"

I really needed to start wearing makeup on a regular basis. "I'm not even thirty!"

"But you're dating that dad guy."

"The chief of police? Okay, yeah, he's a little older than me, but trust me, I'm still fairly cool, and I know a thing or two. Don't put me in the nursing home just yet, 'k?"

"If you say so."

Man, she'd just taken an ax to my ego. "Do you like Atlas or not?"

She smiled as a blush covered her cheeks. "Maybe a little, but still, it's not worth the hassle."

"Here's my unsolicited advice. Tell Atlas you'll go to the dance. Don't let those two stop you from doing something you want to do. If he liked one of them, he would have asked them to the dance."

"I mean, I like him and all, but." She shook her head. "It's complicated."

"Everything's complicated, and trust me, when you're as old as me, it's not any easier."

"Great."

"Pretty much," I said, and laughed. "Now, if I were you, I'd slap a smile on my face, put on my cutest outfit, and go to school like I don't have a care in the world. Screw those girls. They don't deserve someone like you in their lives. Stand up to them by being confident. I promise you, they'll put their tails between their legs and come crawling back to be your friend."

She smiled. "You know what? You're right. Screw them."

I watched her self-esteem find its positive place again. She took off with a poof of air, leaving little sparkles in her place, and I smiled. "Wow, maybe I'll rock the mom thing one day."

I SPENT the late afternoon at the Enchanted working on my novel. I decided the story needed more attention than whatever was or wasn't going on, and I decided to follow my advice to Emma. Stand proud. If Gabe was right, and I was inclined to believe he was, then this wasn't as dramatic as I thought and would all die down soon enough.

Stella walked in. "Hey, what happened to your mental health day?"

"It ended up being a mental health morning, I guess."

She tossed her bag onto a chair and sat across from me. "Care for some company?"

"Your company is always my favorite."

"Oh, I'm telling Gabe."

"Feel free. I tell him all the time."

"And this is why I love you."

"Only that?"

"Well, that and you make a killer sausage gravy."

"I do have many gifts," I said. If she only knew that killer sausage gravy was magically created. I couldn't cook to save my life, or anyone else's for that matter.

Cooper wandered over from the display window and rubbed himself in and out of Stella's feet.

"Hey, sweet boy," she said. She picked him up and held him dangling in front of her face, giving his nose and forehead little smooches.

"Ah, the babes love me."

She dropped my familiar onto her laptop.

Cooper slipped and fell to the ground. "Dang, woman, that hurt!"

Stella stared at me with her jaw hanging open in shock. "Did you do that?"

"Do what?"

"Talk for your cat." She examined my face carefully. "Do it again. I want to see if I can tell."

I took a moment to process what she'd just said. "I...I... yeah, I've been working on it."

"Seriously, do it again."

I glanced at Cooper. He meowed. I hoped he got the hint of what I wanted to say. When he winked at me, I figured he had.

"Give me tuna or give me death."

"You're a jerk," she said, laughing. "I totally saw your lips move."

Cooper wrapped a figure eight through my legs. "I said I'm working on it, not that I'd perfected it." I stood. "Excuse me for a sec, I need to use the bathroom."

"Have at it," she said, and went to work like my cat hadn't just spoken.

I rushed off to the bathroom with Cooper on my tail.

"Well, this just got interesting," he said.

"Okay, no more thinking someone isn't doing all of this on purpose. Logical, experienced boyfriend aside, this is happening."

"You go, girl."

"I'm serious! She heard you speak!"

"Yeah, and she thinks you're good enough to send your voice across the table. Girl is pretty, but she might have lost some brain cells along the way."

"Hey now! Coop, this is serious. We have to find out who's doing this and make them stop."

He stretched out on the sink. "I'm going to need a double dose of energy for this."

"Fish is protein, not carbs."

"Protein sustains energy."

I didn't have enough nutritional knowledge to argue, nor did I care. "Fine. I'll give you two cans of tuna."

"Make it one tuna and one can of sardines, please."

I cringed. "Fine."

"That stink just makes it all so pleasing to the palate."

I didn't have a response for that. "Come on, let's get your food, you weirdo. I have someplace to be."

COOPER FINISHED CHOWING down on his disgusting can of sardines, but he'd barely touched the tuna. He rolled on the Enchanted floor, belly up, groaning something mostly inaudible about a food coma.

"Stella, can you keep an eye on Coop for me? I need to run down the street to talk to Cassie."

"Uh, sure."

"I can watch him too, Miss Abby," Atlas said.

"Thank you." I considered saying something about Emma, but I decided to mind my own business. The girls hadn't stopped in after school, so I hoped maybe the three of them had a talk, and things would be better in the morning. It was possible that was completely off the mark, but I hoped I was right.

Cassie greeted me with a smile and a hug. I hugged her back. I needed to play nice if I wanted to get to the truth. She'd thrown her former best friend under the bus, and granted, I could understand her reasoning, but I was determined to find out if she was the one messing with my best friend to make her archnemesis look guilty.

"So, what can I do for you, honey?"

I'd cast a spell on her before walking into her store. It was risky and a long shot, and I knew that. Manipulating witches magically isn't easy, and a witch with that many years under her belt would be tough as nails. "I'm looking for an essential oil for Stella. Something to help her sleep."

"Oh, is she struggling?"

"Recently, yeah, and I feel bad for her."

She walked over to a shelf located at the far end of the store. After moving a few bottles around, she pulled one from the back, blew the dust off it, and handed it to me. "This should help. It's chamomile and lavender. A few sprinkles on her temples and wrists, and she'll be out for the night."

"Thank you." I headed to her counter. "How much do I owe you?"

"It's on me. Friends like you are rare. I know that from experience."

You can bet they are.

As I walked back to Bessie's place, I magically concocted

a little bottle of essential oils myself. I matched the bottle from Cassie's perfectly, knowing no one would be able to tell the difference. I wanted to check the contents of Cassie's mix and see if she'd given me something other than what she'd said. If I could bust her on that, I might be able to bust her on everything else.

I set my own bottle in front of Stella. "Merry Christmas."

She glanced at it. "It's February."

"Happy Valentine's Day, then."

"You know I never turn down a gift, but we've never exchanged Valentine's gifts, so why now?"

"It's supposed to help with sleep. I figured you could use it."

"Sweet! Thank you!"

"Cassie said just dab a little on your temples and wrists when you go to bed."

She checked her Fitbit for the time. "Is now too early for bed?"

"Not in some countries."

She groaned. "I wish I could, but I've got manuscripts to edit, and a Zoom meeting with a diva client who thinks her writing is Shakespearean." She rolled her eyes. "And I kind of agree."

"Really?"

"Yes. In the sense that you have to read a sentence five times to even begin to understand it."

I laughed. "Nice."

"I wish my clients were more like you."

"No, you don't. I'm a diva."

"You are not! The words just flow from your fingers like magic."

As if. "If that were the case, I'd just snap my fingers and make final drafts appear on the table. No editing necessary."

"Wouldn't that be great?"

"A girl can dream."

I settled in to work, but Stella had to run. "Hey, do me a favor," she asked as she walked toward the entrance.

"Sure."

"Stop that ventriloquist thing. It's creepy."

"I'll do my best." If my essential oil worked, not only would she sleep better, but she'd also never see a magical mishap again.

I set Cassie's essential oil mix on my small dining table.

Cooper sauntered over, jumped onto the table, and sniffed the bottle. "You sure you want to mess with that? It smells like a boys' locker room."

"Ew. It does not. It's soft, feminine smells."

"You sure about that?" He climbed back down to the chair and sat with his teeny little head peeking over the tabletop.

Actually, I wasn't. I hadn't seen Cassie make it, and I hadn't smelled it. I was worried it might do something to me if I opened it, so I kept it closed. "How about we go ahead and find out? Heart of gold, truth be told. To me reveal, what is real." I watched in awe as the bottle top unscrewed itself and the individual ingredients poured into white ramekins. Small pieces of paper appeared in front of each bowl, and I gasped as words were magically written on them.

"Wow!"

Cooper read each out loud. "Havel root, baronian powder, buck salt, toad feces." He grimaced. "Dude. That's some serious stuff."

"Right?"

"Who uses toad feces these days? That's so retro," my cat said.

"That's beyond retro. No one's used that since—"

My eyes shot open. "Holy crap!"

"Right?"

Toad feces went out in the late 1600s, shortly after the tragedy of the Salem trials. Most of the herbs used back then were discarded. Those who survived believed magic and its elements were tainted by their loved ones' blood. They'd sought new options, and after years of hard work, they'd perfected what we use today. And toad feces wasn't on the list.

"Why would Cassie use that?"

"Do you know what it does?"

I shook my head. "I'm still pretty new to this."

"Yeah, but you've researched for your books. Didn't you ever come across toad feces?"

"I've read a lot about various spell elements. You can't expect me to remember it all."

"Dang, girl. You'd fail miserably at Hogwarts."

"What's that?"

"You seriously haven't read Harry Potter?"

I grimaced as I shook my head. "I'm sure the series is great, but it's not my thing."

"Hogwarts is the—forget it. The toad feces is hallucinogenic. Makes people see—"

"Things that aren't really there. Son of a Goddess, Cassie is messing with my best friend!"

"No, Cassie is messing with you."

"How do you mean?"

"My guess is if she knows you've figured it out, she's trying to play with you so you'll drop it." With that, he climbed off the chair and sauntered over to the couch, where he collapsed and stretched out.

"You're not very helpful."

"I'm still recovering from that extra-large can of tuna you fed me a few minutes ago. Give me some time to chill."

"Fine, but I'm going to figure this out while you're snoozing, so don't be surprised if you wake up and I'm gone." I wanted to run the theory by Gabe and see what he thought, but I hated bothering him. I debated doing something else, something I knew I shouldn't. It was a fairly invasive breach of privacy, and totally out of character for me, but I had a sudden urge and didn't really try hard enough to stop myself. I closed my eyes and thought about my boyfriend, chuckling at the term because he was quite a bit older than me, and definitely a man. When his image appeared, I scowled but kept my eyes closed. "Seriously? You're playing pool?"

Gabe glanced up from the pool table, and if I didn't know better, I would have thought he was staring straight into my mind's eye. He smiled. "Do you want me to come over?"

I opened my eyes. "Whoa. That's new."

Cooper's voice was scratchy and deep, like I'd just woken him from a sound sleep. "What?"

My doorbell rang. "That," I said, knowing Gabe was on the other side.

He smiled. "Hey."

I blushed. "I wasn't, uh...I wasn't snooping. I was just wondering—oh, forget it. I was snooping. I just wanted to talk to you about something, but I figured you were working, and I didn't want to bother you if you were busy, and I didn't think you'd—"

"Know?"

I cringed and nodded.

He pulled me into a hug. "I should have called."

"I won't do that again."

He laughed. "Sure you will."

He was probably right, but that didn't mean I didn't feel awful for being a nosy, boundary-crossing witchy girlfriend.

He walked the few steps to my dining table and examined the spread. "Toad feces?"

Cooper groaned. "Please, make him stop. I'm going to hack up a tuna-covered hairball if someone says that again."

There went my desire to eat.

"Cassie created this for Stella. She said it was lavender and something else."

"It's something else, all right. Something to make Stella think she's crazy."

"Cooper thinks Cassie knows I've figured out she's responsible for everything, and she's trying to mess with me."

"Sounds like you've got two very old witches who are kicking their age-old war up a notch. And that notch is you."

"That makes absolutely no sense."

"Think about it," he said as he stepped over to my couch, moved the cat, and sat. "Tell me what you know. I suspect you'll figure out what I'm thinking before you finish."

Right, and two magicals were better than one. I filled him in on everything I'd discovered, what Stella experienced, what I thought, what I assumed, and even what worried me.

"If they were going to have an all-out war, it would have happened years ago. This is just a festering fire that'll blow out soon enough."

"Two words," I said. "Toad feces."

Cooper sat up. "Oh boy." His head jerked and he made the most Goddess-awful sound.

"He's going to throw up," I said, and waved my hand for a roll of paper towels and some cleaner.

Gabe disappeared and reappeared near the table. "That's disgusting."

I laughed. "You get used to it."

Cooper shook his little head. "I told you it would happen." He crawled into a ball, feeling a lot better, I assumed.

The mess gone, Gabe returned to the opposite side of the couch, and we got back to business. Finally, I had a reasonable way to solve my problem and possibly reunite two former friends.

I just had to make sure no one died in the process. And more importantly, that Stella wouldn't remember any of it.

6
___

C at fights are awful, which is the very reason fights between women are referred to as such. But the added element of magic makes them horrible. Most of the time I'd love for Stella to be a witch. It would be fun and, honestly, relieve a lot of pressure for me. Keeping such a serious secret from your best friend is awful, and it feels so dishonest, but rules are rules, and I try to follow them. In this case, I was grateful for Stella's humanness. If she fought back, which was highly improbable, it could only be on a human level, and the damage wouldn't be as bad. What worried me the most was the damage to our friendship, but I hoped I'd come up with a spell to wipe it away and bring us back to normal.

I didn't want to hurt my friend, but Gabe assured me the spell would block the emotional pain, and at some point, Stella would have no idea we'd fought, let alone that I'd started it intentionally. He believed if I wanted to stop being dragged into the middle of Cassie and Daisy's battle, I had to make it appear that it had caused me problems. Maybe then the culprit would chill out.

Before allowing our friendship to take a desperate dive into the pool of bitterness and betrayal, I at least wanted to know if the essential oils I'd provided had helped her sleep. I did a quick check-in—magically, of course—and listened as she snoozed away.

"She's out," I said.

"Great," Gabe said. "So, you're sure you're okay with this?"

"If it's going to fix things, and you promise it won't come back to haunt me, then yes. I'm sure." As sure as I could be, anyway.

He wrapped his arms around me, and I snuggled in close. "You've got this," he said.

I sure hoped he was right.

STELLA CHARGED into the Enchanted looking refreshed and recharged. "That essential oil was the bomb! I slept like the dead!" I glared at her, and her smile dropped into a frown. She sat next to me and put her hand over mine. "You okay?"

I jerked my hand away. "How could you?" I didn't need to fake tears. I was upset over having to betray my best friend, so they fell naturally.

Her eyes widened. "How could I what?"

Mr. Charming flew over and rested on my shoulder. "Mr. Charming loves you." He picked at my head with his beak. "You're a sneaky rat. You're a sneaky rat."

While Stella focused on the parrot, I magically changed things between us. I wasn't proud of myself, but I needed to create a realistic fight to catch a witch.

Bessie stood behind Stella, shaking her head. "Mr. Charming, that's not nice." She stretched out her arm.

"Come, let's give the girls some space." She narrowed her eyes at me, and they practically bled her disapproval.

Stella leaned back in her chair cautiously. "What's going on?"

"Don't act innocent. I know, Stella. I know what you did."

"What I did to—what are you talking about? What did I do?"

I slammed my fist on the table, causing Mr. Calloway and Mr. Jameson to jump in their seats. I stood up and proceeded to give an Oscar-worthy performance. And people thought I couldn't act. "You know what you did, and there's no way I'll ever forgive you!" My voice shook from anger—anger at myself for being such an awful friend, even though my heart knew it was the right thing to do. "We're done! Our friendship is over!"

Stella sat there in shock, her mouth hanging open and her hands shaking as she wiped the tears from her cheeks. Dear Goddess, she didn't deserve this. Stella is perfect. The perfect friend. "What did I do? Just tell me and we can get past it," she said.

I gathered my things. "Please," I said, holding my hand, palm up, toward her. "Just stop. It's done, and we're done. Got it?" I tossed my stuff in my bag and jogged out the door.

Cooper lagged behind. Once outside, I focused my thoughts on my best friend and watched her reaction like a movie in my head. I didn't feel bad at all for snooping this time. I caused the pain, and I deserved every second of watching my best friend devastated because of my actions. If I had to make her suffer, I should suffer too.

"What's going on?" She stood and rushed to Bessie. "What did I do?"

Bessie pulled her into a tight hug. "Honey, it's going to be fine, I promise. She just needs space."

Tears streamed down my face, but I kept watching as my body effortlessly walked to Cassie's boutique.

"I don't know what I did. Why won't she tell me what I did?" Stella cried as she spoke.

"There, there," Bessie said, patting my best friend's back. "She'll tell you eventually. She just needs a little breathing room, honey."

Stella's back stiffened and she jerked away from Bessie. "If she needs space, then fine. I'll give her space." Her face hardened as she wiped the last of her tears from her cheeks. "If she doesn't have enough respect to tell me what she thinks I've done, then screw her. I don't need friends like that." She grabbed her bag and charged out.

Bessie shook her head. "I sure hope you know what you're doing," she said, right into my mind's eye.

Cassie unlocked the door for me. "Honey, what's wrong?"

"Stella and I got into a fight," I said.

Her eyes widened. "What? You two are thick as thieves. What could you possibly fight about?"

"I don't want to say. I'm just too angry." And since she hadn't done anything, I wouldn't invent something and make her look bad, even if Cassie was to blame for it all.

Which I still thought she was.

She caught her smile as it creeped onto her face and turned it into a shocked expression instead. "Stella would never do anything to hurt you. You know that, right?"

I did know that, but I needed the town to believe otherwise. It was the only way to weed out the wicked witch of Holiday Hills. "You don't understand. There's a fine line between love and hate, and I think we've crossed it. There's no turning back." I added a sob for dramatic effect.

"I do understand. You know that. I've been there in a

roundabout way." Her expression turned from sensitive and concerned to devious and deliberate. "But honey, she's a useless human. She has no power over you. Just do your witchy thing and be done with her."

My eyes widened. "Are you saying you don't like humans?"

She shrugged. "They're a means to an end in many cases, but there's no way around them here, is there?"

"If you don't like them, why did you come to Holiday Hills? There are magical towns all over the world."

She fiddled with a bottle of body lotion on a display table. "What's the fun of living in a town full of just magicals? Witches need a certain degree of excitement, and quite honestly, battling with a witch can get boring and even dangerous, but battling with a human is at least entertaining. They have no idea they're being manipulated by magic."

Was she showing me her cards? Why would she be so obvious? Something wicked this way came, and it set up house. But I'd be damned if I let her stay. "You know my story, right?"

She cocked her head and smirked. "About your mother binding your powers and taking away your ability to see magic? Doesn't everyone know? I didn't know it was a secret."

I shifted my weight from one leg to the other and tried to appear completely comfortable. "It's not from magicals."

She walked over to the counter and straightened a pile of marketing brochures. "I understand how it must be for you. Thinking you were human for all these years only to find out you're a witch, and a quite powerful one at that. But the truth is, you're one of us now, and spending your time with powerless humans is wasteful of your gift. You should be expanding your magic, not playing human and hiding it."

"It's you, isn't it?"

"What are you talking about?"

"You're the one doing all of this. You're trying to get back at Daisy for getting you tossed out of Salem, and you're using me and my best friend as some weird parlor trick, aren't you?"

She sighed. "Of course not. I'm not the nicest witch in town, but I'm not like the rumors would lead you to believe either."

She'd done a complete one-eighty, but I didn't trust her. "You sound like a bitter old witch. I don't believe a word you're telling me."

"I'm teaching you a lesson. You're young and naïve, and you think the worlds are filled with goodness and love, but that's far from true. There is a lot of evil in the magical world and even more so in the human world. You may think I'm the one doing all of this, that I'm the one who's acting some revenge upon a best friend from years ago, but that's not true. I'm simply suggesting you pay attention to everyone. No one in Holiday Hills is innocent."

She sounded sincere now. I wanted to slam my head against a wall and scream. Dealing with murderous witches and evil beings was easy compared to dealing with old, bitter witches. I had no idea what to think, and no clue how to act.

Cassie sensed that. "I know you think I'm responsible for what's happened."

"You gave me an essential oil filled with toad feces. What am I supposed to think?"

Her right eyebrow went up. "Toad feces? I haven't

touched that since—what makes you think I gave that to Stella?"

"Because it was in the mixture you gave me to help her sleep. You did it so she'd see things and think she was crazy. You want to ruin my friendship just like you ruined yours."

"Where's the bottle? I want to see it."

I held out my hand and the bottle appeared. "I pulled the ingredients. Havel root, baronian powder, buck salt, and toad feces. Not one drop of anything sleep-oriented."

She carefully took the bottle and examined it. She removed the top and poured a few droplets onto a tissue. The tissue dissolved in seconds. "Oh dear."

"Stop trying to hurt my friend!"

She closed the bottle and then blew it up in a tiny explosion. It disappeared, as did the flame. "I promise you, I did not give you that mixture. Someone must have switched out the bottle."

"And I'm supposed to assume that's Daisy, right?"

"I suggest you talk to her."

I didn't want her to know I hadn't really confronted Daisy with any of this. I just didn't feel Daisy was capable of anything she'd been accused of. And whether Cassie did something to upset her best friend or not, I couldn't imagine Daisy holding onto that anger for hundreds of years. "Ginger was alive during the trials too. Could she be doing this?"

"Ginger?" She shook her head. "She knew I didn't do anything in Salem. She was on my side. She even agreed to talk to Daisy for me, but of course, Daisy wouldn't hear any of it. Daisy made that oil, Abby, and she found a way to switch it so you'd give it to Stella. All to blame me and get me thrown out of Holiday Hills, I'm sure of it."

I wasn't as sure as she was, but I intended to find out the truth.

GINGER GREETED ME WITH A HUG. "You look like something a crow discarded on the street, sugar. You okay?"

That wasn't specific at all, I thought. I kept that tucked in the back of my mind for possible use in Adelle's story. "It's been a long morning."

"Can I help you?"

I glanced around the store, but the place was empty. "Can we talk about Daisy and Cassie?"

She blinked. "What about them?"

"Their fight back in Salem. I know things happened, but Cassie hasn't provided too many details, and I haven't really talked with Daisy about it. I was hoping you could fill me in."

"What exactly do you want to know?"

"What happened that would cause Daisy to let the townspeople think her best friend was a witch?"

She sucked in a deep breath. "Oh, Goddess, there is so much to that story."

"I'm all ears."

"I'm afraid it's not my story to tell."

"Ginger, someone gave my best friend toad feces."

She tilted her head. "That hasn't been used in years."

"Exactly. And it came from Cassie's shop, but she swears it's not hers."

"And she blamed Daisy."

I nodded.

"Well, that is concerning, I'll give you that. I can't see Daisy doing that, though, not to sweet Stella. And really, what would be the point? Why would she want to hurt your friend like that?"

"Maybe she didn't. Maybe it was Cassie."

"Why would Cassie want to?" She sprayed water on a Bonsai tree sitting on a small display table. "Has Stella done something to upset her?"

"Not that I'm aware of. And full disclosure, Cassie swears she has no issue with me or Stella, so I'm not sure why she would do it."

"Cassie has been known to harass other witches. I believe I told you that?"

"That's why I'm asking about what happened. Please, I'm pulling straws here to figure out how to make this stop."

"I'm not sure I can help you, but I will say I wouldn't trust either witch. They were both so angry. I wouldn't put it past them to go at it after all this time."

"And you think Cassie is responsible?"

"What makes you say that?"

"Because you immediately said she was a problem for Salem when we talked about her before. You said you thought she was causing trouble here."

"Did I?" She pressed her finger to her lip. "I don't recall that."

My next stop was Daisy's, and I was ready to throw my cards on the table. I needed answers, and beating around the bush wasn't the way to get them.

Cooper showed up there at the same time. "Funny seeing you here," he said as he made a figure eight between my legs.

"Got a bug up your behind?"

He turned to check. "Do I?"

I shook my head. "That was a play on words. What I meant was, what's got you out and moving around?"

"It's my job."

I nodded. "All right, then. What brought you here specifically?"

"Just call me psychic."

Familiars and their charges, as Cooper liked to call me sometimes, have a special bond, and it's often referred to as psychic. Because they're charged with protecting us, they have a sixth sense focused on us, or someone or something intent on doing us harm. It had its advantages, but there were times it wasn't convenient.

"I was just at Cassie's," I said. "It's like she's got a split personality or something."

"You say that like you just realized that."

"I knew she was a little, I don't know, curt, I guess, but this is more than that. She went full-out wicked witch of the west. She said humans are useless, but then she made this total shift and was all nice again. It was weird."

"She's never had a human give her a box of tuna for Christmas."

I smiled. Stella gave Coop his own box from Costco every year. She won points with him forever for that. "I'm not sure that would make a difference."

As Cooper started to speak, my cell phone rang. I dug it out of my purse. "Hold that thought," I said as I stepped away to take Gabe's call. "Hey, what's up?"

"I've got some news."

"About what's happening in town?"

"No. About Texas."

"As in the state of?"

"Yes, ma'am."

"You're going away, aren't you?"

"I'm afraid so, but that doesn't mean I can't pop in now and then for a visit."

"Like every night?"

He laughed. "I'm sorry."

"Is everything okay?"

"It will be."

"You can't tell me anything, can you?"

"Had you taken the job with the MBI, I would be taking you with me."

"I'm sorry. I write about mysteries and crimes, I don't want to deal with them in real life."

"Yet you're busy trying to solve a case in Holiday Hills on your own."

"Because I feel like it involves me."

"I know, and I think you're adorable for that."

"Will I hear from you soon?" I asked.

"As soon as possible," he said. "In the meantime, know I'm thinking of you. If you need me, I'll be there."

"Thank you, that means a lot."

Cooper groaned. "Your main squeeze leaving you?"

"Only temporarily."

"Hmph."

"What?"

"Maybe it's another witch."

I rolled my eyes. "It's Texas and it's for work."

"You're so gullible sometimes."

I stared down at my Burmese familiar. "What're you implying?"

He stood on his back legs and shrugged his little front shoulders. "Texas is witch country. Those babes wear tight jeans and tight T-shirts with guns and stuff on them."

I furrowed my brow. "Your point?"

He gave my wardrobe a once-over. "A warlock like Gabe might prefer that to leggings and a big sweater. You're not really showing your stuff, you know?"

I winced. "I...I don't need to show my stuff! Gabe isn't that kind of man, er, uh, warlock."

"You keep thinking that."

"Listen, you little eighties throwback or whatever you were." I waggled my finger at him. "Just because you liked your witches in revealing clothes doesn't mean that's Gabe's thing, and it certainly doesn't mean he's going to dump me for some western witch who likes guns."

"Okay."

I stared at him.

"I said okay. Stop with the death stare."

I opened the door to Daisy's, then turned around and said, "You're so not getting the good stuff for lunch today."

"Not surprising."

Daisy rushed to me and smiled, but it faded when she saw my frown. "Oh heavens, what's wrong?"

"It's nothing," I said. My frown was genuine but directed at my snarky familiar's attitude. "Nothing I want to talk about, I mean."

"Are you sure? Sometimes it's good to get things out in the open. If anything, talk to Bessie. She's family to you, and she can help, I'm sure."

"I'm not sure anyone can help me."

"Oh dear, is this about what's happening in town with the power outage and such?"

I shook my head. "I'm not worried about that anymore."

"Then is it Stella? Is she okay?"

That wasn't what I'd expected her to say. "She's fine. Why do you ask?"

"Oh, she was in here yesterday acting a little discombobulated. I haven't seen her that way before. I thought maybe she was sick or something."

Interesting. If Stella had been in Daisy's, she hadn't mentioned it to me, but she didn't normally tell me where she went. Then I suddenly remembered I'd cast the spell to make Stella think we were fighting. "I haven't...I haven't spoken to her much. We're kind of in a fight."

Her eyes popped. "What? You two are thick as thieves!"

"That's what I thought too."

"Oh, sweetheart, do not sweat the small stuff. Whatever's happened, it'll pass. Good friends like you two are hard to find. Trust me, I know. You should never walk away from a good friend, even if they've hurt you, without at least getting everything out in the open."

"Thank you." I wanted to ease into what I knew on my own terms, and I didn't want it to come off as disingenuous. I'd gone from thinking Daisy was the sweetest witch around, to thinking she was evil, to knowing she'd almost had her best friend murdered by fire, to thinking again, as I stood there talking to her, she was the sweetest witch around.

I really had no idea what to think, so I switched the subject. I was genuinely worried about Daisy's business. I've always loved Blooming Blossoms, and I wanted the store to remain open. "How's business?"

She sighed. "It's the same. I did my books last night, and I don't think I'll make it to spring. With all the chaos in the world, you'd think people would want flowers in their homes, both human and magical, but it's not happening. I've even got special flowers no one else can find. Marigold Blooming Roses are my particular creation, and they've stopped selling. I don't understand. They used to be my most popular flower."

I patted her shoulder because I didn't know what else to do. "I'm sorry. It's bound to pick up."

"If it doesn't, in less than a month I'll be broke."

"I'm so sorry."

"I've even considered casting a spell over the humans in town. I know it's not appropriate, but it's for the greater good, not just my business. Flowers bring happiness, and if I cast a spell to get more business, would that be so bad? Creating happiness for people through magic?"

"Things don't work that way, Daisy, but I sure wish they would."

Cooper jumped onto her counter and nibbled on a sprig of leaves framing white roses in a vase.

"Cooper, no!" He looked at me like he didn't give a darn what I said and went back to his snack. I picked him up and set him on the ground, then pulled a twenty-dollar bill out of my purse. "I'd like to buy that, please."

"Oh, don't be silly. No one will notice the nibbles."

"I'd still like to buy them. I could use the happiness, just like you said."

"You're a dear," she said.

"May I ask you a question?"

"Sure."

"Did something happen between you and Cassie back in...in Salem?"

She blinked. "You've been talking to Ginger, haven't you? She likes to tell everyone Cassie was kicked out of Salem because of me, but that's not the truth. Rumors are awful. I wish people would stop spreading them."

I wouldn't verify who told me what, and though I hated being dishonest, I felt it was best to keep my sources private. "I saw your names in a book about Salem. I've been doing some research for a book I'm working on and I saw a drawing too. One of the people in it looked a lot like you."

She raised an eyebrow. "That's interesting. Yes, Cassie and I were friends, but witches change, and we've gone our separate ways."

She was very calm, almost too calm. "Does it bother you that she's come here?"

"Why would it bother me? The trials were hundreds of years ago. What's done is done. We've both moved on."

"May I be honest?"

"I hope you would be."

"It's amazing to me that you were...that you have..." I didn't know how to say it without lessening the effect of what she'd gone through.

"That I was around during the trials?"

I nodded sheepishly.

She smiled. "There are a lot of us from then. Ginger and Cassie are the only others in Holiday Hills, but we're everywhere."

"Did you know Ginger back then?"

"Everyone knew Ginger. She was as big of a gossip then as she is now." She raised her eyebrows and flicked her head to the right. "We didn't associate with the same magicals, but we were familiar with each other, and I know her family suffered from the trials too. We were teenagers back then. It was a long time ago, but I do believe Ginger was the one who told me about Cassie and..." She furrowed her brow. "You know what, I can't remember the boy's name now. Goodness, it's been so long, I can't even remember what boy my best friend tried to steal from me."

"Can you tell me what they were like back then?"

"Magicals?"

"No, Cassie and Ginger."

She furrowed her brow. "What's going on?"

"I can't really say."

She crossed her arms over her chest. "Abby Odell, you can't ask that kind of question without offering an explanation."

I could, and I had, but it wasn't respectful to say that. "Okay, you promise to keep this to yourself? I don't want it to get around."

She nodded.

"Sometimes, when I write characters in my stories, I model them after people I know. Those two have been around more lately, and they intrigue me. I thought I'd use one of them as the villain in my next mystery."

She laughed. "Well, if that's the case, then I suggest you make someone like Cassie the killer. She's the only one of the two who's self-centered enough to use her magic to harm people."

Given her earlier calmness when discussing her former best friend, that surprised me. "Wow."

She shrugged. "Okay, so maybe I am a little bitter. I guess when it comes to matters of the heart, witches can be as crazy as humans."

My mouth hung open as I scrambled for something to say.

"Honey, I'm not saying Cassie would actually commit murder, if that's where you're going with your story. I just think of the two witches, she's the most, I guess, resentful and prone to doing things good witches shouldn't do. I've experienced it firsthand. Ginger was a gossip back in the day, but that's nothing compared to trying to steal your best friend's boyfriend."

"Do you think maybe you're a bit biased about that?"

"I sure am, and I deserve to be. We let a man get between

us, and even though we were young and stupid, neither of us behaved as friends should. I'm just as ashamed of my own behavior back then as I am of hers, but I haven't done anything to hurt her."

"What about telling the townspeople she was a witch?"

"Did Cassie tell you I did that? I promise you, I was angry, and I may have told people Cassandra Mayflower was a horrible person, but I would never, ever, tell them she was a witch."

Then why did Cassie and Ginger tell me she had?

7

Cooper hung close as I walked back to the Enchanted. A gust of wind had swept through, picking my nine-pound familiar straight off the ground and sending him several feet in the air before I snatched him as he sailed back to the sidewalk.

"That was close," I said. "You're lucky I was paying attention. My head is full of so much right now, I can barely focus."

"If you'd feed me more, I could gain a few pounds of muscle, and you wouldn't have to worry about me."

"You do know the average Burmese weighs between six and fourteen pounds. You're in the middle and a perfectly healthy weight. You should be thankful. If I fed you more, you could end up dragging your middle on the ground."

"That's rude."

"So is telling me my significant other is going to dump me for a Texas hottie!"

"The truth hurts, babe."

"Watch yourself," I said with a grin. "I have opposable thumbs to open tuna cans, you know."

"And lovely thumbs they are."

"Right."

The wind picked up again, sending clumps of hair across my face. "This is getting old," I said as I spat out stray hairs caught in my mouth. Sparkles of light zipped by me and formed humanlike shapes in front of me.

Emma, Britney, and Amber huddled close together and giggled.

I glanced at Cooper. "Looks like the war has ended." I hoped Emma had stood up for herself and decided to go to the dance with Atlas after all. The best way to shut up a bully was to not let them see you afraid.

"For now," he said, and kicked up his speed. Cooper's legs were the length of my middle finger, and he rarely went anywhere fast, unless a can of tuna was involved, or, oddly, I played 80s pop music. His metal-head tendencies caused him to run and hide when he heard anything by Rick Springfield, Rick Astley, or the like. I happened to love the stuff because my mother played it all the time. But when I was in trouble or he was hungry, he went into full-throttle familiar mode, and his teeny legs deserved nothing less than the theme from *Rocky* playing along.

"Where are you going?" I whispered.

He crooked his neck back and said, "Shh. Gimme a sec."

I shrugged and picked up my pace. I didn't want to appear creepy or nosy as I approached the girls, so I slowed just behind them. Cooper had already passed them and darted to the right, straight into the Enchanted.

"Hey," Britney said when she heard me behind her.

The other two turned and smiled. Emma's eyes widened for a second, but she recovered quickly. I smiled at her, hoping she'd realize I wouldn't say anything about our previous conversation.

I checked my watch. "It's late. You guys are going to get detention."

They laughed. "It's a teacher workday. There's no school."

I nodded. "I guess I'm a little old to know that."

Emma smiled. "It's okay, you're pretty cool for an old person."

Ouch, I thought, though I pitched her the softball on that one. "So, let me guess." I pressed my forefinger to my chin. "Atlas is working now, and you're going to hang out at the Enchanted."

They laughed.

"We are so over Atlas," Amber said.

"Yeah, warlocks are so out of touch," Britney added.

I eyed Emma. She looked away.

"Well, keep your voices down," I said with a smile. "I've got a deadline on a book, and I'm behind."

"You're a writer?" Amber asked.

I nodded. "Sure am."

"Dude, that's cool. I hate reading, but I'll read what you write because I like you," she said.

Finally made it to the cool crowd in high school. Goddess knows I wasn't in it when I was their age. I laughed. "When it's out, I'll get you a copy. Y'all can pass it around."

"Cool," Britney said, though her tone reflected anything but.

Atlas stepped out from the kitchen and greeted me with a smile. "Hi, Abby."

"Teacher workday today," I said.

The girls were already at a table pretending to ignore Atlas. I caught a quick look between him and Emma and tried not to smile. She'd definitely changed her mind about the dance.

"Uh, yeah," he said. "I, um...can I talk to you for a minute, like, in private?"

I raised an eyebrow. "Sure."

"Cool," he said.

I followed him into the kitchen. Bessie was on the phone placing an order, but she waved when she saw me.

"What's up?" I asked him.

"So, we have this, like, dance coming up, and I was wondering if you could, you know, give me some...help me, uh..."

I pursed my lips to stop myself from smiling. "Are you asking me for girl advice?"

He blushed. "I don't even know. I want to make it special, but I've never been to a dance before, and the girl I'm going with is a magical, so, you know, I, like...it's a lot of pressure."

"You're taking Emma?"

He raised his eyebrows. "How'd you know?"

"She might have mentioned it."

"Whoa. She's talking about it? Her friends were mad, so she wasn't going to go, but I told her not to let them bully her like that."

"You're a smart guy, Atlas."

His shoulders sank. "Not smart enough to know how to make this the best date she's ever had."

I smiled. "Just the fact that you're worried about that means it's going to be special. And just because she's a magical doesn't mean she needs something over and above what every high school girl wants on a date."

"I don't even know what that is. I've never really been on a date. Not this kind, and it's really important."

He really liked Emma. The poor kid was going to need to wear a lot of antiperspirant the night of the dance. He was so nervous just talking about it his face was sweating like crazy. "Listen, she likes you, and it's pretty obvious how much you like her. That's all the magic you're going to need. Bring her a corsage, preferably for the wrist because the other ones are really hard to pin on a dress, and just be yourself. That's all it's going to take."

"You sure?"

"Trust me, I may be ancient, but I know a thing or two about dating."

He smiled. "You're not ancient."

"I'll take that," I said, and grabbed a bag of potato chips as I walked through the kitchen door.

The girls all stared at me as I put my stuff on my table. I pretended I didn't notice.

Cooper walked over and sat on the chair beside me. He glanced at the girls, then eyed me suspiciously. "Well?"

"Well, why the rush to get to the Enchanted?" I asked.

"I smelled sardines."

"Gross."

"You don't understand the delicacies of life."

"Obviously."

The girls whispered to each other but kept their eyes on me. I smiled at them. "It wasn't about any of you," I finally said. "Bessie's birthday is coming up, and he wanted to talk about that."

The excitement on their faces disappeared.

"That's sweet," Emma said.

"We made a pact," Britney said. "He's off limits."

Oh boy. She hadn't stood up for herself, and things would get ugly when they found out Emma felt differently. Bessie walked over to my table. I'd already flipped open the book about the Salem witch trials and was searching for anything I could find about Daisy and Cassie.

"That book isn't going to tell you anything you don't already know," she said.

"Sometimes you have to read between the lines."

"That seems like a polar opposite approach." She sat down and scooted her chair toward mine so she could get a good look at the book.

I glanced around the store, making sure the other magicals weren't paying attention, then wisped my hand across the old pages and said, "Times before, show me more."

The book pages flipped several at a time and then stopped near the end. I read the passage out loud, whispering it so only Bessie could hear. "The witches were inseparable, but all of Salem understood the betrayal would come, and it would bring fierce, wicked damage to the betrayer."

Our eyes met, and Bessie's mouth hung open. "Do you think that's about Cassie and Daisy?"

"I don't know. What do you think?"

She leaned back in her chair. "I can't imagine why that would be so important then. They had bigger things to worry about."

"Females are like tigers when males are involved. It doesn't matter if they're human, animal, or magical. The claws come out and it makes the news. That stuff is timeless."

"Maybe," Bessie said. "But I think you need to dig deeper."

"What do you mean?"

"I understand that women have battled over men for years, but it's hard to believe a childish battle would be such a big deal when witches and women were burning at the stake."

Cooper stretched and meowed. "When you two figure it

out, let me know." He hopped off the chair and sauntered to the display case to lie down and snooze.

"With all due respect, I think you're wrong. I think it was a big deal, but I also think I'm missing a link in the story. If I figure that out, then I'm sure this will all make sense."

"Any clue what that missing link might be?"

"Not a single one."

"Then go back to the beginning and see if you can find it."

I thought long and hard about everyone in town. Only Daisy, Ginger, and Cassie had lived during the trials, but that didn't mean someone didn't know what happened with Cassie and Daisy and was messing with them just because they could.

It also didn't mean this wasn't somehow about me, though I couldn't figure out the connection. Was someone playing with me and Stella because they thought it was funny? I replayed the last few days in my mind. Whose face flinched when I did magic? Who groaned when I walked into a room? Who acted nicer than expected? I really couldn't pick anyone specific. Every magical in town seemed generally nice toward me. Sure, some might have whispered behind my back, but if they had, I wasn't aware. I felt like Emma being ousted from her friend group, only she knew about it, and they let her back in. Maybe my social circle included a Benedict Arnold, and if it did, it was time I found out who that was.

I didn't think this was about me, but whoever dragged me into it did so for a reason, and I was determined to stop this whole mess.

8

The magical world is full of rules and regulations. Witches aren't allowed to cast spells or use their magic for selfish reasons, but it happens. We're also not supposed to look into the future, change fate, or force people to do things they wouldn't otherwise do. Again, just because we aren't allowed doesn't mean it doesn't happen. The problem is, magic and karma are first cousins, and when someone messes with magic, karma comes running to the rescue.

Last week I watched two witches battle it out over a red velvet cupcake. It progressed to the point of violence, and when karma stepped in, all I could do was laugh. The cupcake ended up soaring across the Enchanted, doing a double loop around the place, and then coming back to hit Mr. Calloway smack in the nose.

It was the last cupcake in the place, and Bessie assured the witches she wouldn't be making more anytime soon. If you're wondering why the witches didn't just make their own, you haven't had one of Bessie's red velvet cupcakes.

I knew casting a spell to find out who was creating

havoc in my life was risky, but I was desperate. I couldn't win a war against an opponent I didn't know. I may have been a powerful witch, but I didn't have a whole lot of experience in witchery. I wanted to fix whatever was happening, and if using magic was the key, then that's what I'd do.

I stopped at Ginger's for some supplies.

She greeted me with a smile. "Hey, Abby, back so soon?"

"I need some supplies."

Her eyes lit up. "Are you planning something exciting?"

"Yes," I lied. "Do you have any snail trail, basil root, and peppermint?"

Her mouth twitched. "Snail trail? You know how powerful that is, don't you?"

I nodded.

"Well then, let me get the items. I have to mix the snail trail. It'll be about ten minutes. Is that okay?"

"Sure. No problem at all."

Snail trail sounded disgusting, but in truth, it was a pleasant-smelling essential oil mix of sea leaves, algae, and jellyfish saliva. Okay, that part was disgusting, but as a whole, it was a good essential oil, and perfect for what I needed to do. I wandered around Ginger's shop, smelling the scented candles and admiring the hand-painted vases and other items scattered throughout. I sampled a few candies, which were delicious, and read a short blurb taped to a display about the magic of essential oils. Everything it said, from how their scents trigger memories to witches using them for hypnosis, was true, but humans wouldn't even give it a second thought because they don't believe in witches or magic.

Ginger finished the snail trail and placed it in a bag with the other items. "I'm so grateful you're doing this," she said.

"I have been so worried about our cozy little town. If something were to happen, it would devastate everyone."

"What do you mean?" I handed her my debit card.

"The power outages, the weird darkness for humans. Why is that all happening? Who would do that to Holiday Hills?"

"Oh, that," I said. "Yes, that's why I've decided to do something. I can't guarantee it's going to work, but it's worth a shot."

She slipped a small container in the bag, then folded the top and stapled it shut. "I'm giving you a little something I've created that adds a little kick to my spells. I think it might help."

"Thank you," I said, then went home and got right to work.

Cooper jumped on the table and coughed. "What stinks?"

"I picked up some essential oils at Ginger's place."

"Seriously?"

"I need them for a spell, and she's got the best in town."

"But you can't trust her."

"I can't trust anyone right now."

"What about Bessie?"

"Coop, I appreciate the concern, but I need the strong stuff, and Ginger's got it."

He sighed. "You're making a mistake."

"Possibly so, but I'm out of options."

"All right then." He hopped down, pranced to the couch, and snuggled in for another nap.

I set five candles in the shape of a star on my small table. I lit each one and placed small glass ramekins beside them, then climbed on top of my kitchen counter and opened the cabinet above my refrigerator. I dug through a collection of candle holders and partially melted Yankee Candles from a previous Christmas until I found what I was looking for. Removing the small box, I opened it and checked inside to make sure its contents were safe. Then I opened the bottom drawer next to the oven and removed a small bottle of avocado oil mixture I'd created a few weeks ago before carrying the two items back to the table.

I opened the bag from Ginger's and placed the items in a line on the table. I took a ramekin I'd set aside and placed it in the middle of the star, then poured three droplets of each oil into the individual ramekins while repeating, "I come seeking truth."

Once I finished with the oils, I opened the small box and removed three strands of my mother's hair. Of all the witches I knew, she was the most powerful. I never saw her perform magic, but since her passing and the unbinding of my own magic, I've been able to replay memories and see where she'd cast spells and manipulated events magically. Addie never used magic for personal benefit, but she also believed rules were just guidelines and found ways to work around them in both life and magic.

I put the three strands of my mother's hair in the center ramekin and whispered, "Oh Goddess of witches past, bless me with your powers and show me the truths to stop the danger surrounding me." I'd tried to think of a cutesy rhyme, but I didn't have any more time to waste, so I just got to the point.

I picked up each ramekin and poured its contents into the center one, watching as they covered my sweet mother's hair and whispering, "Please, Mom, please."

When I poured the snail trail into the mix, a small fire ignited. I watched as my mom's hair fizzled away, catching my breath when it completely disappeared. My heart raced and my eyes fogged over. I heard Cooper say something, but I couldn't quite make sense of his words. I tried to stand, but my legs were weak, and I fell to the ground. Everything went dark.

"Hello? Ground control to Major Tom?"

I opened my right eye and stared straight into my familiar's face. I groaned.

"Wakey, wakey!"

I pushed him off me, feeling like I'd spent the night downing shots of tequila while doing some crazy exercise boot camp. Everything hurt. Every muscle, every bone, every nerve. My head pounded and I craved Taco Bell, and I never craved that stuff. "What happened?" I forced myself to sit up. It was painful. "Why do I hurt so much?" I glanced around my dark apartment. "What time is it?" When the realization that I'd probably been out for hours hit, I panicked. "The spell! Did something happen?"

Cooper hopped onto the couch and nodded. "Oh yeah, baby, something happened all right."

I crawled to the couch and dropped myself onto it. I pulled the blanket out from under him and wrapped it around my shivering body. "Can you just cut to the chase and tell me what you saw, please? I'm in too much pain to beg."

He crawled to me. "After you cast the spell, you did this weird jerking thing, you know, like the *Peanuts* gang dance, and fell out of your chair. I was going to move you, but you kept freaking me out, so I figured I'd let you work through your issues on your own."

I rubbed the back of my neck. Was it possible to fall two

feet to the ground and crick my neck somehow? It sure felt like it. "It was so weird," I said. "Like a movie."

"What? Your slow-mo fall to the ground? It was pretty non-eventful, if you ask me."

"No. The spell. It must have put me in some sort of trance, and it played out things in town like a movie."

"Lemme guess, you were the star."

I rolled my eyes at the cat. "No, I wasn't in the movie, I just watched it."

"So, I was the star."

"Absolutely."

"I sense sarcasm in your tone."

"You should." I was able to smile and not feel like it used every ounce of energy even though I was exhausted. "I saw people doing things." I rubbed the back of my neck again, but it didn't ease the pain. "Stella talking to Gabe. And Gabe! Gabe was flitting in and out of scenes. It was like he was a part of it all. Oh! Cassie and Daisy were in it too. And Cassie was—" My jaw dropped. "Oh, my Goddess, Cassie slipped something into Daisy's drink at the Enchanted!"

Cooper's ears perked. "Describe 'something.' Creamer or something like toad feces?"

I closed my eyes and tried to recall the film as it had played in my mind's eye, but I couldn't bring up what I needed. I could only recall the scenes in small flashes. And there were a lot of scenes, several weeks' worth of events that happened in Holiday Hills. "Bessie and Stella planned a party for me. Did you know that?"

He nodded. "Canceled it, though."

"Why?"

"Because you went all drama queen about celebrating anything after your mom died, and they didn't want to upset you any more than you already were."

"I appreciate that."

"Don't tell me. Tell them. You were a pain in the butt back then."

"Was I?"

"I thought about running away."

"Oh, whatever." Another part of the spell came to me. "Atlas! That poor kid."

"What?"

I bit my lip. I wasn't going to share Atlas's coming drama. It wasn't my business, and it felt so wrong seeing something that had nothing to do with me. Spells don't always turn out how we plan, which is one of the major downsides to being magical. "Never mind." I dragged myself off the couch and headed to the kitchen for a big glass of water. I felt so dehydrated, I guzzled two glasses in seconds.

"You figure out what you wanted to know?"

I sighed. "I'm not sure. I saw a lot of strange things, but the most alarming was seeing Cassie slip something into Daisy's drink. It's odd, though—it was at least last year, maybe earlier."

"How do you know?"

"Because Daisy's hair was still dark."

He gave that some thought. "That was about a year ago."

"You pay attention to that kind of thing?"

"I'm a familiar. We're all-seeing."

"Oh, geez."

He smirked. "Anything else?"

"Yeah, weird stuff, but nothing that said who is doing things to my best friend. I saw Mr. Calloway leaving cards in people's mailboxes. Mr. Charming sneaking out the back of the Enchanted and flying over to the park. Gabe doing some sort of karate moves to—"

Cooper interrupted me. "Hold up a sec. Did you just say the parrot left the building?"

I nodded. "Crazy, right? He flew right out the back door and to the park." I pressed my lips together and then smiled when the scene flashed in my head. "There's a bird there! I think Mr. Charming's got a girlfriend!"

"Dang! The parrot's got it goin' on!" He fell onto his backside and licked his paw. "Didn't see that coming."

"Stop." I poured myself another glass of water and carried it back to the couch along with a bag of pretzels. "I don't recall seeing anything about this whole mess. I don't know who's causing the magical illusions, who made Stella hear you talk, how she saw the broom, or anything." I plopped down on the couch with a groan. "This stinks."

Cooper jumped up next to me. "Just because you don't remember it yet doesn't mean you won't eventually. Give yourself time to process it all. Just close your eyes and start at the beginning."

So, I did. After popping a pretzel into my mouth, I did my best to recall the details. Cooper respected my efforts and didn't say a thing. Twenty minutes later, I still didn't know if anything that had happened was about me or Stella, but I did learn that Ginger and Daisy had been trash-talking Cassie all over town. Cassie was so upset, she'd accidentally cursed them both, significantly reducing the amount of traffic in the other women's boutiques for over a week. I almost felt bad for Daisy, especially since she'd been so upset about her business being on the verge of closing, but I couldn't be empathetic. She created her problem and deserved what she had coming. Whatever happened between them back in Salem should be dead and buried just like the poor souls who lost their lives. Let the dead rest and the evil die. It wasn't hard. Or at least it shouldn't be.

I could vaguely recall something with the high school trio, but it was too much of a blur to make sense. Spinning buildings, flashing lights, loud music? It all felt like it represented the dance until it went dark, and I couldn't make out anything more from it. I decided they might be worth a watchful eye just to see if I could trigger some sensible information in my head. Besides, I felt sorry for Emma. She didn't deserve to be treated differently than anyone else, especially by the girls she considered her friends.

I was frustrated that I couldn't find a suspect in the ever-confusing mystery of who's that witch and what's really going on? Was it too much to ask the powers that be to do me a solid and show me the truth? Apparently so.

The spell left me feeling a strong pull to Daisy and Cassie and wanting to help them fix the deep wounds that ruined their friendship. At first, I thought it was karma, since I'd cast the spell to upset my friendship with Stella, but the more I thought about it, the more I realized the connection between the magical mishaps, the darkened sky, and the centuries-old battle between the two witches had to be connected. Fix their friendship and things would go back to normal, I told myself.

How I was supposed to do that, though, was beyond me.

Yup, two hundreds-year-old witches with pent-up angst toward each other. Nothing at all complicated.

I could sneak around town and spy on my neighbors for days and not come up with anything. I could skirt the issue, pretending I was some magical private eye who dug into the minds of others and solved world mysteries, but meh. We all know that's a bunch of hoopla. I might have magical powers, but even they couldn't help me. I decided to give up my sneaky ways and just put myself out there using the truth. After all, didn't the truth set us free?

9

It was bright and early on a cool February morning. I woke up smiling and even humming "Let's Hear It for the Boy" from *Footloose*. My mood had shifted in my sleep, though I suspected Gabe's midnight visit had something to do with it. He'd popped in just to kiss my forehead and tell me he was thinking about me, then off he went, saving the magicals or whatever it was he'd been tasked to do.

Bessie looked surprised when I walked into the Enchanted thirty minutes before my normal time. "Uh, hey, Abby! What's got you here so early?"

I tilted my head. "Why are you being so loud?"

She eyed the restroom sign and whispered, "Stella's in there."

My jaw dropped. "Oh." I'd set my bag on the counter, but I quickly picked it up and made myself invisible.

Stella walked out and examined the combination café and bookstore before proceeding toward the counter. "Did I hear you say Abby's name?"

"What?" Bessie tried to appear innocent. "Oh! I was

talking to Mr. Charming. I told him Abby's late. He was, uh...he was asking where she is."

Stella's eyes turned glassy. "Oh."

"Sweetie," Bessie said as she walked toward my best friend. "Things are going to be okay; don't you worry."

"I don't even know what I did. She wouldn't even tell me."

"Abby's got a lot on her plate right now. Just give her some time. You know this book is wearing on her."

"All the more reason to lean on me. She knows how important she is to me. She knows I'd never intentionally do anything to hurt her."

I wanted to crawl under a rock and stay there forever. My best friend was hurting because of me, and I hated myself for it.

"Of course she knows," Bessie said, wrapping her arm around Stella again and hugging her close. "I'll talk to her, okay? I'll help straighten things out. In the meantime, just give her some space. I'm sure this has nothing to do with you."

"Thank you. And yeah, I'm going to give her some space. I've decided to stay at my dad's for a few days. It's just weird being here without talking to her every five minutes."

I felt like a stalker listening in on my best friend's pain. As a kid I always thought being the fly on the wall would be exciting, but I was wrong. It felt dirty and ugly, and awful.

"I'll let Abby know," Bessie said.

"Thanks, Bessie. I appreciate it. Will you tell her I love her too?"

She smiled. "Of course I will, sweetie. Now you tell your daddy I said hi and make him a good hot meal. I worry about your dad."

I reappeared as soon as Stella was out of sight. "That was awful."

Bessie narrowed her eyes at me. "You heard all of that, I assume?"

I nodded sheepishly. "I'm a horrible friend."

"No, you're protecting your best friend from a possible threat. You're a wonderful friend. It's just a tough way to go about it, that's all."

"Thank you," I said. "And I appreciate that you two were going to have a party for me, but thank you for not following through."

She smiled. "You bet."

"I'm going to fix all of this, I promise."

"I have no doubt you will. You know where to find me if you need me."

"Thank you," I said, and headed out to figure out what was happening once and for all.

I STOPPED at Cassie's first. The store was dark, which was to be expected since it wasn't close to her opening time. I flicked my hand and opened the door. When I stepped inside, I felt the vibration of the silent alarm shoot through my body. "Cassie, it's me, Abby Odell."

Cassie appeared before me, walked over to the alarm box, and tapped in a code before switching on the lights. "What's going on?"

I placed my hand on her shoulder. "Come with me," I said, and we both disappeared.

Seconds later, we appeared at Daisy's place. She was already there and filling the coolers with new flowers. When she saw me, her eyes widened. "What's going—"

Her eyes narrowed at Cassie. "And what is she doing here?"

"Witches, this has gone on long enough." I turned toward the door, then waved my hand and locked both locks. I steadied myself, turned around, and smiled. "Witches battle, witches fight, it doesn't matter who's wrong or right. Take these hearts and make them one, keep them bound as the earth circles the sun."

"No!" Cassie screamed. She tried to disappear, but my spell bound her to the store.

"Why are you doing this?" Daisy asked.

"Because." I walked toward them. "You two are holding onto something that happened hundreds of years ago. For what? You were best friends. Don't you think that means something?"

Cassie stomped her foot. "She wanted me burned at the stake!"

Daisy's eyes widened. "I did not! I was upset because you were trying to steal my boyfriend." She paused and pursed her lips. "And Ginger kept filling my head with these horrible stories about what you were doing. She saw you with him. She told me everything. All I did was tell a few trusted friends, but I did not tell anyone you're a witch." She wiped a tear from her eye. "And I don't even remember the boy's name now."

"You don't even remember his name, but you remember me wanting to steal him? That's crazy," Cassie said. "Why would I want to steal any of your boyfriends? I wasn't lacking in the pursuers department."

"Oh, so you're saying you didn't think what's-his-face was good enough for you? Is that it?"

I laughed. "Are you two listening to yourselves? You're fighting over something that happened so long ago neither of you can remember the details. Me and my best friend are fighting now, and even I'm mature enough to understand in the whole scope of things, this fight will likely mean nothing. You've had several hundred years to put this behind you, but you're both too stubborn, and honestly, you're acting like high school girls."

They both stood there grimacing with their arms crossed over their chests. It would have been funny if they weren't so serious.

"You may not like what I'm doing, but frankly, my dear witches, I don't give a damn. In spite of what you think, I'm doing this for you, because I know what it's like to love a friend so much and then feel their loss. This isn't about betrayal. Of course Daisy didn't want you burned at the stake, Cassie." I threw my arms in the air and the lights flickered unintentionally. "You were her best friend! She was hurt, and it's time the two of you figure this out and fix it."

"But she's done things," Daisy said as tears fell down her cheeks.

"I was never interested in your boyfriend. I'm not sure why you would believe Ginger. But you've hurt me. I was pushed out of my family's home, the town where I grew up, and those rumors followed me for years. That's what they were, Daisy. Rumors. Rumors you never cared to talk to me about," Cassie said.

"This is exactly why I'm doing this," I said. "Now it's time to work through it all. I'll be back to check on you in a bit. But I'm not kidding around. I'm going to keep you two here until you work this out, so you better get started." I raised my hand to make myself disappear, but before I did, I said, "Now I've got to pluck the weeds from this town once and for all. Wish me luck." I whipped my hand in a circle and landed outside Daisy's.

Two minutes later I bumped into Atlas rushing down the street with a breakfast order. "Hey, you have a minute? I need to talk to you about something."

"If you don't mind walking with me to Mr. Calloway's place. I've got his bagel sandwich. Bessie said he's feeling under the weather this morning."

"Not a problem," I said, and walked beside him. "About the dance."

He stopped and stared at me. "What's wrong? Did she say something to you?"

I shook my head. "No, no. That's not it. I just...well, I learned you might not have some of the skills necessary to, uh, you know, actually dance."

"Did you talk to my mom?"

I bit my lip. "Let's just say I can sense some things."

"I wasn't worried, but now I am."

"Listen, don't panic, this is fixable. It's just that I'm pretty sure at some time during the dance Emma's going to actually want to, you know, dance."

He rang Mr. Calloway's doorbell. "She is? What am I going to do?"

"YouTube is your friend. Trust me, I am one hundred percent confident it will help you. Just go online and watch some videos, and I don't mean things like John Travolta from *Saturday Night Fever* or the New Kids on the Block stuff. I mean today's stuff and slow dances. Not the waltz or anything, just basic slow dances. Just watch and practice. You'll be fine."

"What's New Kids on the Block?"

"A very old boy band from the eighties. I think they're senior citizens now. Which is exactly my point. Don't dance like that."

He laughed. "I think I can handle it. I play football and basketball. I should be able to dance. Right?"

I had a feeling those guys all thought dancing would be easy, too. Just in case, I whipped up a little spell and tossed it at the kid. He didn't deserve to embarrass himself around a girl he really liked, especially one who was willing to go behind her friends' backs to be with him.

I said a quick hello to Mr. Calloway, then snapped myself back to the Enchanted.

Emma, Amber, and Britney were already there. I smiled at them, then quickly walked into the kitchen. I'd planned to make myself a coffee to go, but Bessie had already done it for me.

"For you," she said, handing me the cup. "No sugar, extra cream."

"You are a good witch."

"So I'm told." She winked at me.

The girls sat at a table with an old book opened between them.

"Can you believe it!" Amber exclaimed. "She could be your twin, Emma! Seriously. Look at her."

I wandered over to them, playing myself off as somewhat interested but totally casual, though truth be told, I was dying to see what she was talking about.

"Hey," Britney said. "Want to see something crazy?" She flipped the book toward me. "That drawing looks almost exactly like Emma."

I examined the drawing. Britney was right. I noted the title of the book. "*Witches of Salem*? Is this one of Bessie's books?" I eyed Emma, but she wouldn't look at me.

"It's my mom's," Amber said. "She was looking at it last night and showed me this picture. Totally wild, right?"

I looked at Emma again, but she still wouldn't make eye contact. "It's probably a very distant relative."

Emma finally made eye contact. "My mom said we had family in Salem, so it probably is."

"I mean, wouldn't, like, all of us have family there?" Britney asked.

Her question was rhetorical, but I decided to answer anyway. "Actually, no. My family comes from a long line of witches, but I don't believe they were in Salem."

"Really? That's weird," Britney said. "My mom says some of the witches who escaped the trials came this way, and apparently, some of them are actually still alive."

Emma's eyes widened, and Amber gasped.

"Oh, that's just an urban legend," I lied. "That's been going around since before I was born, and I've yet to meet anyone who's that old. Imagine what they'd look like?"

"My mom says they cast spells and use oils and creams to keep their youthful glow, whatever that is," Britney said. "I bet some made themselves babies again so they could start over. How cool would that be?"

Emma sank a little in her chair.

"I write this stuff, and trust me, it's all fiction." I glanced at Emma. "Hey, I have that thing for your sister, but it's in my apartment. Can you come get it with me?"

She pushed herself up from the table. "Uh, yeah, sure."

I grabbed her arm and rushed her to the back of the Enchanted. "That was you, wasn't it? Oh, my Goddess! What're you thinking?"

Her jaw stiffened. "I'm not doing anything wrong."

"You manipulated yourself to be a child again, and you're hundreds of years old! How can you possibly be okay with that?"

"It's not what you think. I didn't do it, and don't you

think if I could fix it, I would? What sane witch would want to go back and start over as a baby and go through all this teenage stuff again?"

She had a point. "Okay, tell me what happened, but make it quick."

"My family went into hiding during the trials."

"Many witches did."

"And when my mother gave birth to my little brother, she hemorrhaged and almost died, so she healed herself magically."

I tapped my iWatch, suggesting she speed it up. I had things to do.

"And basically, my mother was caught. She was killed. My grandmother couldn't care for me and my siblings. She was old and weak, and broken. She sent us to live with another family, but eventually we were all separated, and I ended up with a family who moved far, far away. It's Montana today, but back then it was an empty, awful place. I was enslaved to the family, and especially the man who was supposed to be my father. Albus was a wicked, wicked warlock who never should have been near children. He had this presence about him, and no one believed a word I said. They thought his charming good looks, blond curls, lean masculine body, and sweet words showed his true character. They were so wrong. I was lucky, and I escaped, but I couldn't survive on my own. I wasn't a strong enough witch to live out in the wild like that."

"I don't understand how this brings you here."

"When I was on my own, I met this man, a warlock of sorts, though I can't say for sure. He cast a spell over me, and the next thing I knew, I was a child again, living here in Holiday Hills with a wonderful family. He saved me. He gave me a life I could handle and love. So, you see, it's not my fault. I didn't do this."

Atlas walked back and stopped short. "Oh, sorry. I didn't know you two were back here." He pulled the black beanie from his head, revealing his blond curls.

I'd seen them before, but it all made sense. My blood rushed through my veins. I stared at him, my entire body shaking, then glanced at Emma. When I saw the hate filling her eyes, I whisked my hand toward the boy in front of us. "Atlas, be gone!"

He disappeared.

I grabbed Emma's shoulders. "No! You will not hurt that boy! Do you hear me, Emma, or whatever your name is? You will not hurt that boy!"

She laughed. "Just try and stop—"

A metal cage appeared around her. "Don't think I haven't done this kind of thing before," I said, and sent her and the cage off into the ether until I had time to deal with her.

"Atlas, you'll be fine," I whispered. "I promise."

I wasn't sure if Atlas was Albus, or if Emma was exacting some kind of sick revenge on him because he was the next best thing, but either way, I wouldn't let her hurt him.

Mr. Charming was busy distracting the other two girls when I walked back to the main area of the Enchanted. "Mr. Charming is sweet. Mr. Charming is sweet."

Cooper glanced at me from the counter and rolled his little eyes. I caught my breath and smiled, but I knew Cooper could tell something was up.

"Where's Emma?" Britney asked.

"Oh, she had to, uh, bring that thing to her sister. I'm sure she'll be at school later." I doubted she'd make it to school that day or any other day, but what they didn't know would arouse suspicion.

Bessie peeked out from inside the kitchen. "Abby, can we chat for a minute?"

I walked back there casually, as if I didn't have a care in the world, though I was shaking to my core at the knowledge that Emma wasn't who she claimed to be and was probably a very powerful witch. When the door closed behind me, I blurted out everything. "I'm sorry. I had to send Atlas off for a bit, but he's fine. I promise. Once I figure out what to do about Emma, I'll bring him back. Emma's a witch, and she's going to—I don't know if she's involved in all of this mess or what, but I'm going to fix it, okay? I promise, I'm going to fix it."

"Honey, take a breath, slow down, and tell me again. What did Emma do?"

I filled her in one more time.

She gasped. "And you think Atlas is Albus?"

"He matched her description, and when he walked toward us and took off his hat, the hate in her eyes was clear." I shook my head. "I can't believe I missed all this. What's wrong with me?"

"Nothing's wrong with you. You weren't focused on them, and why would you be?"

"She's got to be involved in this, but Atlas, or Albus, or whatever his real name is, he's got a lot of explaining to do too."

"If he's a bad warlock, I don't want him back here."

"And I'm with you on that, but until I have all the information, I don't feel comfortable just banishing him because someone said he's evil. Look what's happened to Daisy and Cassie? I can't be responsible for ruining someone's life because of a rumor."

She smiled. "I'm proud of you. You're becoming more and more like your mother. She'd be so happy."

"I'm hoping she is. I have to run. I've got to get back to the witches and see how they're progressing. Busy! Busy! Busy," I said. For the time being, at least, Atlas was safe, and Emma wasn't going anywhere. One problem at a time, I thought. I disappeared in a flash of smoke, which I thought was pretty darn cool.

Daisy sat behind her counter tapping a pencil on the granite. "Well?"

Cassie paced the small store, her head down and her hands behind her back. "Athena Carrington?"

"Nope. She was a mean old witch, but she was too lazy to destroy a clock."

"You're probably right."

"What about Cordelia Montgomery? She hated that church. Remember how she'd walk past it and hold her ears because the bells were so loud?"

Cassie laughed. "Everyone did that."

I appeared next to Daisy. "How's it going here, witches?"

She jumped at the sound of my voice. "Abby Odell! You scared me."

Cassie laughed. "You're still so jumpy. I thought you'd have grown out of it by now."

Daisy blushed as she smiled. "That kind of thing sticks, and I blame you."

Cassie smirked. "That I'll claim, but only because it's still the funniest thing I've ever seen."

They both laughed. It was progress, and my heart swelled. "What are you talking about?"

"When we were teenagers, Cassie used to sneak up behind me and tap my shoulder. It scared me so much I would jump at least a foot in the air every time. One time I landed wrong and sprained my ankle. I fell right to the ground, and in a fresh pile of dog feces. Cassie didn't let me live that down."

"I loved that dog," Cassie said through laughter and tears.

"At least one of us did," Daisy said. She laughed and cried too.

"See? Look at you two! I'm so happy you're finding your way back to each other."

They smiled.

"We're bonding over memories," Cassie said.

Daisy nodded. "I know now Cassie would never hurt me, and I believe she knows I would never hurt her."

I stared at Cassie and then at Daisy.

"What?" they asked in unison.

"I know about the trash-talking and the other things you've been doing to each other. Have you addressed any of that? Because if not, you need to. You can't have that stuff coming back to haunt you after you've fixed all of this. If you're going to do the work, you have to do all the work."

"She's right," Cassie said. "And I own the fact that I gave you something to impair your magic, but it wasn't—"

"You what?"

Cassie's bottom lip quivered. "I...I'm sorry. I was mad because I'd heard you and Ginger were trying to have me kicked out of Holiday Hills, and I...I just wanted to—"

Daisy's shoulders sank. "I'm sorry. You're right. We were trying to hurt you. Ginger was saying all these awful things."

"Was this a while ago, before you changed your hair?" I asked.

Daisy nodded. "And she's been doing it again recently. "She swore Cassie was the reason my store's sales have been declining. She blamed her for everything happening to me, and I was so wrapped up in my pain, I couldn't see straight. I believed her."

"I didn't do anything to hurt your sales. I wanted to stun you, not damage you permanently. My spell was a simple one to confuse your powers. I never did anything to your store."

"She's right," I said. "Sort of. Her anger and pain were so strong that she couldn't effectively cast the spell, so it ended up impacting your sales, but it wasn't intentional."

"It wasn't, Daisy. I'm so sorry. I should have behaved better from the start."

"Why would she want you two fighting?" I asked.

"Ambrose! That was his name," Daisy said. "The boy. His name was Ambrose. He was such a sweet young man, and he was nice-looking, too. Little blond curls at the ends of his hair. And strong. So, so strong."

"Ambrose? You sure it wasn't Albus or Atlas?"

She pursed her lips. "I think it was Ambrose."

"I think she's right," Cassie said. "And you know what? I think Ginger might have liked him at one point too!"

Their eyes met, and it was like a bomb exploding between them. Sparks flew, lights flickered, the room shook. Cooler doors opened and flowers fell off the shelves. I leaned against the counter to steady myself.

"That witch!" Cassie screamed. "It was her! It was her all along!"

"How did we miss that?" Daisy asked. "How could we be so blind?"

Cassie gasped. "Abby, you have to stop her. She's doing all of this to make us look bad. Please, stop her!"

Daisy agreed. "I just didn't see it!"

"*We* didn't see it," Cassie said. "And look what's happened! You're fighting with Stella. The two of us have been at each other's throats for Goddess knows how long, and it's all because that woman is a wicked, miserable witch who just wants everyone to be as miserable as she is. Find her. Stop her!"

I rushed outside, then stopped to catch my breath and settle my racing heart. Only about a third of what they said made sense, but I knew I was missing something. If Ginger had liked Ambrose, did she think making the other two witches battle would make him like her? What was the point of her behavior? What was I missing?

"Hey," a voice whispered from just around the corner. "How you doin'?"

I glanced over but no one was there.

"Psst. Down here."

A shiver ran up my spine as I aimed my eyes toward the ground. "Are you talking to me?"

The large gray rat nodded. "Yeah, I'm talking to you. You think I'm talking to myself?"

Another rat with almost the exact same coloring appeared next to him. I knew they were magicals, but ick. Magic or no magic, rats were rats, and they scared me.

"So yeah, we wanna thank you for, you know, getting our gals back together," the first one said.

"Excuse me?" I asked. I backed away as they scurried closer.

"Looks like she's got a problem with us," the second one said.

"You got a problem with us?" the first rat asked.

I stepped back and shook my head. "Who, me? I mean, no. No problem."

"We ain't rats. We're familiars. What's not to love?" the second rat asked.

"We got sharp claws, and we eat trash. She don't look

like the kind of gal who goes for that. She looks like a lady," the first rat said.

I shivered. "It's not that. It's, uh, well, it's nothing personal. I'm just not a fan of rodents in general."

"We ain't either," the first one said. "You think we picked these bodies? You think we like the urge to dumpster dive for food scraps and drag it along the ground before we eat it? Huh? Do ya?"

The second rat stood on his back legs and raised his right front leg. It would have been cute if it didn't make me queasy. "I know I miss a good rare steak and a big bowl of spaghetti with a splash of sauce. And it's called sauce, not gravy. Don't know why people keep calling it gravy."

"Gravy goes on biscuits," I said.

"Now that's what I'm talking about!"

The first rat, who I'd determined was the boss, whacked his muscle on the arm, knocking him back on all fours. I felt like I was watching a Disney version of *The Godfather*.

"Speaking of steak, you wouldn't mind whipping us up a few, now would you?"

I smiled at the muscled rat, but then I remembered what exactly I was talking to. "I'm sorry. I'm pretty busy at the moment."

"Yeah, that witch? She's long gone. We've been tracking her for years and she keeps losin' us. Now that right there is what you call a sneaky little rodent."

"Hundreds of years, she's been doin' that," rat two said.

"Feels like thousands," rat one said.

"Some days," rat two said.

I raised an eyebrow and chuckled. "Are you familiars or a bad comedy act?" I felt a teeny bit more comfortable near them, but not enough to settle in for a snuggle.

"Did you just call us stupid?" rat one asked.

My eyes widened. "No, I asked—no." I swallowed hard. "I don't think you're stupid."

"Good, because we got connections, you know, and we're not afraid to use them," rat two said.

"For cryin' out loud, Joey, shut your piehole. That ain't the way this stuff works no more. We're not working for Tony no more. This is the big time. We're tryin' to thank this lovely young lady for helping our charges." He shook his head. "Lemme apologize for my friend here. He likes to talk tough, but he's a big softy." He laughed. "I mean it, touch him. Go ahead, I dare ya."

"Thanks, but I'm good."

"All's we're tryin' to say is thanks for reuniting our witches," he said.

The second rat snickered and rubbed his needle-thin claws together. "Yeah, it's good. It's good. We been trying to do that for years now, but they're, you know..."

"Stubborn old bats," rat number one said.

"My pleasure," I said. "It's been nice chatting, but I've got to go."

"Be careful," the first rat said. "They're right about that Ginger. She's up to no good."

"Got it," I said as I rushed away. When I looked back to make sure they weren't following me, they were both standing on their hind legs and waving at me. I shuddered. "Blech. I'm not a rodent person."

"We heard that," one of the rats hollered.

Ginger's store was locked, and the lights were off. I crouched down close to the sidewalk, held out my hand, and said, "Holiday Hills map."

The map appeared on the ground. I then asked for my crystal pendulum and it popped right into my hand. I asked it to show me Ginger's location.

The pendulum spun in a wide circle around the map, slowing as it moved closer to the paper. When it dropped like a magnet and stuck, I examined it carefully and gasped. "Goddess!" I blinked my tools back to my place and rushed back to the Enchanted.

10

I burst through the door and stopped short when I saw Bessie sitting at a corner table with Ginger, chatting away like she wasn't even the slightest threat.

She smiled and waved me over. "Hey, sweetie, you look flushed. You okay?"

I took a deep breath. Bessie was one of the smartest witches I knew. There was no way she would hang out with a wicked witch or even a potential wicked witch without a reason. She had to have a plan. A good plan, too, because I sure didn't. I just stormed in ready for a fight with a witch whose power was hundreds of years old and probably pretty darn strong.

"I'm good," I said, staring straight into Ginger's eyes. "Just left Daisy and Cassie. They've worked things out."

Ginger blinked. Yes! She was visibly shaken. Step one of my *flying by the seat of my pants* plan complete.

"I did some investigating into their situation, and after speaking with their very dedicated familiars, I learned their fight was about a situation neither of them caused. They were both manipulated into thinking things were different,

and they've spent all this time missing out on their relationship. It was truly invigorating to watch them reunite. Makes
me appreciate my relationship with Stella so much."

Bessie kept her eyes locked on me.

"Where is Stella, by the way? I tried to call her, but it
went straight to voicemail," Ginger said.

My toes curled, and my jaw tensed. Stay calm, my logical
side said. Then the protective side of me sucker-punched
the logical side and knocked her out. Don't mess with my
bestie, witch, she said. You won't know what hit you.

That wasn't true. She would know what hit her, because
I'd be smiling right at her as it happened.

"She went on a trip," Bessie said. "An editors event in
Scotland. She'll be gone for a while."

I smiled. Bless you, Bessie, for having my best friend's
back. "She didn't add the overseas option to her cell plan, so
she won't be taking calls."

If Ginger thought we were lying, she didn't show it. I
didn't trust her, though, and I wasn't willing to rest on my
laurels. "So, Ginger," I said as I pulled out a chair and sat
between the two witches. "I didn't realize you were so close
to Cassie and Daisy back in the day. That must have been
hard, seeing the two women fight about something that was
all a lie."

Cooper appeared out of nowhere and did a figure eight
through my legs. I leaned to the side and petted his head.

"I got you," he said in a voice only I could hear. I gave
him a little tap to let him know I understood.

Ginger steadied her hands on the table, a witchy sign
that she was ready to pounce if need be. I set my hands on
the table too, and Bessie followed along. The cards had been
dealt and it was time to see who folded first.

"I barely knew them," Ginger said.

"Really? That's not what they said."

She shifted in her chair. Bessie watched her carefully. Cooper jumped onto my lap and shoved his little head between my arms. Mr. Charming flew over and planted himself on the back of the only empty chair at the table.

"Mr. Charming sees all."

The Enchanted's door swung open and a large raccoon charged in. He stood on his hind legs as his head shifted back and forth. When he saw all of us, he scurried over and planted himself right next to Ginger.

Oh boy, I thought. Rats were bad enough, but they weren't generally mean, just focused on their ultimate food goal. Raccoons, on the other hand, could be pretty nasty little boogers when necessary. As the familiar of a wicked witch, it would also align with her feelings, and that wasn't good for anyone. The thing weighed at least twenty pounds, well over Cooper, and I worried if they fought, Cooper wouldn't be able to carry his weight in the battle. We had Mr. Charming, but I'd never seen him do anything physical, even when mimicking Clint Eastwood. His claws were threatening, but the raccoon could easily scoop him up and toss him into a wall.

Goddess, this could be a mess. What had I started? This just showed that spur-of-the-moment planning wasn't smart.

"Nice familiar," Bessie said. "Unfortunately, raccoons aren't allowed in the café."

Ginger laughed. "What? Are they against the department of health standards or something?"

"As a matter of fact, they are," Bessie said. She stared at the masked mammal.

"Yet the bird and cat are allowed."

"I make exceptions for family."

"I see," Ginger said. Her tone was calm, but her body language bordered on combative.

I decided to take the bull by the horns. I didn't want to drag our familiars or Bessie and Mr. Charming into a battle that would definitely be ugly and most likely harmful. Bessie's powers were strong, but she wasn't part of this. This was on me, and it was between me and Ginger. She'd messed with me and my best friend long enough. The witch was going down. "Ginger, have I done something to upset you?"

She narrowed her eyes at me. "Why do you ask?"

"I think you know, and I'd like to do whatever I can to mend our broken fences." Play nice, but prepare to strike.

She stared at me, then directed her eyes to Bessie and Mr. Charming. "Cage," she said as she waved her hand at them. "Trapped and bound, hidden from all even if I fall!"

My heart stopped as Bessie and Mr. Charming disappeared into thin air. "No!"

Ginger laughed, then set her hands back on the table. Cooper snarled and hissed. Her raccoon stood on his hind legs, preparing to come to her defense, but I sent him flying across the store and into a bookcase filled with hardcover classics. The case fell and books crashed onto him. Cooper charged over and shot under the books. For just a few seconds, both Ginger and I stared in awe as books flew and pages ripped, flying all over the store.

"What did you do to Bessie?" I screamed. "Bring her back!" I stood and slammed my hands on the table. "Now!"

Ginger sneered. She stood and shoved her hands toward me. I fell back and tumbled over the chair. "Where's my sister?" she screamed. "When I get her back, I'll think about letting you have your Bessie back."

I pushed myself off the ground. "What? I...I don't know what you're talking about!"

She threw back her head and laughed, and then her body morphed into the redhaired college student who worked at the Picnic Café in Dahlonega. "Where's Emma?"

I stepped back. Cooper hissed nearby. I flipped around and screamed as he soared through the air and landed hard on the cement floor. "Stop it!" I flicked my hand and shoved the raccoon hard into the pile of books.

Ginger took that opportunity to charge me magically again, knocking me over with a force unlike any I'd felt before. I shot backward and landed in the pile of books, their hard spines feeling like sucker-punches I couldn't hide from. I screamed.

"Where's Emma!" Ginger stood over me, her hands poised to do something magical. "Bring her to me or die, witch!"

I turned toward Cooper. I was grateful he was in one piece, and to keep it that way, I needed to get us out of there. I wasn't prepared for Ginger's intensity, and I needed to figure out what the heck was going on. "Cooper!" I screamed. "With me!" I blinked and the two of us landed safe and sound in the middle of Goddess only knows. It was warm, and there was water, and Cooper rushed to it, drinking it like he'd been dehydrated for days.

"Emma is Ginger's sister? Ginger was the college girl working at the Picnic Café? How was any of this possible, and how did I miss it?"

"Stuff happens," Cooper said. He breathed deeply. "This is going to hurt tomorrow."

The ground shook. I stared at my familiar, lifting us both into the air so we were hovering over the grass. "Here she comes!"

"Let's do this, baby!"

I blinked and seconds later we were at Ginger's store.

"What're we—why did you—oh dang, are you running like a chicken?"

"What?" I shook my head. "No! Go to Daisy's. Find the rats. They'll help us fight them!"

"Rats? It's my genetic makeup to hunt and kill them, not be buddies."

I glared at him. "Cooper!"

"Bad timing, I know. My bad."

"Go!"

He took off. I cleared the center of the store with a wave of my hand, then willed Emma's cage to appear.

She stood inside it, shaking the metal bars and speaking words from a language I didn't understand.

"Bind her!" I yelled. "Take her power and send it away. Leave it there until I say!"

She screamed. "No!" Her body shook, and she collapsed to the cage's ground.

My body surged forward. I tried to gain my balance, but the force was too strong. I fell against the cage, hitting my head so hard I saw stars.

"Bring her to me!" Ginger yelled. "Or your Bessie and that bird will pay!"

I rubbed my head and stood, but my legs were shaky, and I couldn't maintain my balance. I reached for a display table and leaned onto it. "Why are you doing this?"

"You ruined everything, and now you'll pay!"

I took a deep breath, then released it. I began saying a spell to bind Ginger's powers too, but she stopped me before I could finish.

"Witch, you've got nothing on me!" She pushed her hands toward me again, and I fell back onto the display table. Each time I tried to get up, she would push again, and again, I'd fall.

"Stop it!" I screamed. I magically threw candles and essential oils at her in a rapid flow. The bottles burst, and when the oils combined on the ground, sparks erupted. My eyes widened.

Ginger waved off the fire. "You'll never win!"

I pictured a pair of steel handcuffs and wrapped them around her hands. She stared down at them and laughed. I added another, and another, and another. It wasn't much, but she'd have to take the time to remove them. I tossed a few around her legs too. It gave me a chance to catch my breath and figure out what the heck was happening and why. I walked over to Emma as Ginger struggled to remove the cuffs. She wasn't as powerful as she wanted me to believe, and using all that power at once exhausted her. She was sweating and red, and her energy was lapsing.

"Why?" I asked Emma. I narrowed my eyes at the cage and lifted it off the ground, slamming it down hard and scaring her, hopefully enough to start talking.

"You'll never understand," she said.

"Try me." I glanced back at Ginger. She'd removed two of the handcuffs and was close to getting the rest off. "And make it quick."

"It was Atlas, or Albus, or whatever he goes by. How blind are you? He professed his love to my sister, and then suddenly he's with Daisy. She ruined everything, and she needed to pay."

"How could you help her? You were just a child!" I whipped another set of cuffs onto Ginger's wrists.

"I will destroy you!" she screamed.

I'd calmed a bit and gathered my strength. "Try it," I said, tossing her into a cage where I could see her, but not close to her sister. I took two steps back, whisked my hand in a circle, and said, "Powers that be, protect me. Place a shield around my space and keep these evil witches off my case!"

A soft white glow encircled me. It sparkled and shimmered, and hummed loudly. "This needs to stop. Whatever anger and resentment you're carrying, you have to let it go."

"That will never happen," Ginger yelled. "Atlas was mine, and Daisy stole him from me."

"He abused your sister years later. Why would you want him back?"

"You're so naïve. I don't want him back. I want him dead."

It all began to make sense. "He was seeing you in secret, wasn't he? And when you found out he wanted Daisy, you let her think Cassie was the girl he'd been with. Those witches think this is about them, but it's not. You didn't want Daisy or Cassie to pay. You just used them to get back at Atlas."

"And it worked too. Like magic," she said, laughing. "He ran like a scared little boy."

"And then he wound up caring for your sister."

"He didn't care for me," Emma said. "He abused me."

"How did you know it was the same warlock from Salem?"

"I just did," she said. "Magic never forgets."

Ginger laughed. "When we found each other again, we knew what we had to do."

"You were planning to hurt Atlas and, what, blame it on Cassie or Daisy?"

She laughed again. "And we were close."

"Until I came around. And all the play with the power? And Stella!" Anger rushed through me, and I wanted to zap them into oblivion right then and there. "You tried to make

Stella think she was crazy! For what? To distract me so you could finish your stupid plan? How dare you!" I shoved my hands out in front of me, and the two witches slammed into the backs of their cages. "Nobody hurts my best friend!" I took a deep breath and forced myself to calm down. The whole reason they were in this situation was because of anger and revenge. I wouldn't let myself sink to their level. I might get close, but I wouldn't drown with them.

Emma screamed, "It's all your fault! He has to die!"

Teenager or not, she knew how to pitch a fit. And I'd gotten it all wrong from the start. This wasn't about me. It wasn't about destroying witches. It was about a cheating warlock and a really ticked-off pair of magical sisters.

There really was a fine line between love and hate.

Emma shook her cage and screamed, "Let me out!"

I blinked and the cage door swung open.

She stared at it for a second and then ran to her sister's cage. "Open it," she said, screaming louder than before. "Free her!"

I shrugged, then waved my hand. The cage opened. As Emma stepped inside and reached for her sister, I slammed the door shut.

She turned around and screamed so loud I couldn't hear myself think. "No! We must finish our plan!"

I closed my eyes and focused on the two witches. I pressed my fingers against my temples and repeated, *Send them back to where they belong,* over and over, calling upon the witches of Salem for help. "Send them back, witches of Salem! Take them away and bring us back to before things went astray! Clear the witches of space and time and return our town to simply divine!"

Ginger shrieked as she threw her arms in the air. "No!"

A sudden burst of fire lit up around the cage. Ginger's

screams intensified as the fire exploded. Emma and I screamed too. The flames pushed me backward, sending me sailing through the air and smacking against the back wall of the boutique. Oils, candles, and candlesticks crashed to the ground, hitting me on the head in the process. I yelled, doing my best to cover my head with my hands. "Cooper! Help!"

Flames engulfed the small boutique. I screamed louder as the ceiling collapsed and debris fell on top of me. I tried to get up, but I couldn't. I was trapped under something big and heavy, and I was too weak to move it. All the emotions had drained me physically and magically, and I lost all of my energy. I could die there if I didn't do something, and do it fast!

I closed my eyes and screamed as loud as I could, "Cooper!" When I opened my eyes, a lion stood before me, fire surrounding him, almost touching his golden mane. Standing beside him were two large wild boars, grunting and snorting, pushing the lion to act. And he did. He roared with such ferocity the room shook. He slapped his massive claws at the heavy piece of debris on top of me and sent it flying across the store. I screeched in fear of falling victim to those deadly claws. One by one each piece trapping me soared across the room as fire spread throughout the store.

"The fire!" I screamed. "I need to stop the fire!" I struggled to get my arm out from under me. If I couldn't use my arm, I couldn't stop the flames. I was exhausted. My head hurt, and no matter how hard I tried, I couldn't get my arm to do a thing. "My arm! It won't move."

The lion stepped closer, ripping one last board away from me and gently nudging my arm. With the softness of a grandmother caring for her first grandchild, he lifted my arm. "Now," he growled. "Do it now."

I focused every ounce of energy and power I had on my index finger. "Enough," I said. My finger moved just a teeny bit. "Enough!"

The fire disappeared.

"Ginger! Emma!" I tried to scream, but the words came out as more of a whisper. I'd used all my energy, all my voice, to move that finger. "Get them!"

The lion turned around, ready to pounce, but they were gone.

My spell worked. He turned back around and nodded once, then bowed his head and shrank back to his original size.

The wild boars snorted and grunted loudly, then warped back into the small rodents I'd grown to like more than I would have imagined.

I blinked twice and then laughed like I'd never laughed before. "You, my familiar, will never want for tuna or salmon again. I promise!"

Cooper meowed and then sauntered away like he hadn't just saved me from a fiery death. "Man, I'm starving."

"And you two," I said to the rodents. "Steaks on me tonight." I felt immediate remorse for saying that. I'd happily get them steaks, but I couldn't have them at my house for dinner. I had my limits.

I ARRIVED at the Enchanted bright and early knowing Stella would arrive earlier than my normal time just to avoid me. I held Bessie's hands and spoke with a desperation so strong, the fire from last night seemed years ago. "You sure this is going to work?"

"I'm positive. I made sure she came home late last night,

and I promise you, she doesn't remember a thing. You just sit yourself down and stop worrying. I've got this."

Sending Ginger and Emma to wherever they had gone meant all of their magic in Holiday Hills ended. After it all went down, I'd dragged myself the few hundred feet from Ginger's store to see if Bessie was back at the Enchanted. I was so grateful to see her sitting inside with Mr. Charming on her arm, I literally fell to the floor and sobbed.

That night I told her everything about Ginger, Emma, and Atlas, and she'd been as shocked as me. My arm hung limp as pain vibrated from my neck to my fingertips. I was able to move it a little more as the night progressed, but it wasn't enough to do what was necessary to make things right with my best friend. As much as I'd wanted to cast a spell to reunite me and Stella, I still didn't have the strength. I looked into Bessie's eyes as tears fell down my cheeks.

"Don't you worry," she said. "I told you, things will be fine."

"What if she remembers?"

"Oh, sweetie." She pulled me close. "I'm good; you have to trust me on that. Stop worrying. It's going to be fine. And I promise you, you'll get your strength back, both the magical and physical. It's going to take some time, but it'll happen."

I was about to say I hoped she was right, but Stella came in, and time stopped. At least for me. The look of sadness on her face crushed me more than when the ceiling fell on me. Her hardened eyes made me even weaker. My bottom lip trembled.

"What happened?" she asked. She rushed over to me and wrapped her arms around me, crushing my injured arm in the process. I didn't jerk away. Even though it hurt, I laughed it off and smiled as tears welled in my eyes. "Hurt arm here!"

She broke off the hug. "Oh geez! I'm sorry. I wasn't thinking. When Bessie called me last night and said you'd had an accident, I wanted to rush home right then and go straight to your place, but she insisted you needed to rest." She examined me closely. "Are you okay? What about the other guy?"

"The other guy?"

"Bessie said his car was totaled too. Was he hurt?"

I glanced at Bessie. She smiled. "Oh, he's fine."

"Good." She helped me to my regular table. "How are you going to work on that book? You hate dictating."

"I'll be fine," I said, and I knew I would be with my best friend back in my life.

Bessie handed Stella a cup of coffee. "I'm using a new cream. Let me know if you like it. If not, I'll swap it out for the old stuff."

Stella sipped the drink. Twinkles of lights wisped around like a small tornado. As quickly as they appeared, they disappeared. Stella lost her balance for a second but caught herself. "I don't know what I'd do without your coffee," she said to Bessie. She sat next to me. "That essential oil was the bomb, by the way. When I got home last night, I slept like the dead." She heaved her bag onto the table and opened it. "I brought it for you just in case you need it. And given the way you look, I think you're going to."

I honestly couldn't remember what oil she was talking about, and which witch I got it from. Just to be safe, I took it and stuffed it into my bag. I'd dispose of it later but tell her I used it all, lavishing it with tons of loving adjectives to sound believable. I held out my good hand and she took it. "I may look bad, but I feel one hundred percent awesome."

Mr. Calloway walked in and coughed. "Big night last night, huh?"

Bessie shot him a look that shut him up fast.

"What's that about?" Stella asked.

"Oh." I blushed. "You really must have slept like the dead. There was a fire at Ginger's place last night. I couldn't sleep, you know, because of the accident, so I went for a walk and saw the flames. I tried to get inside, but I couldn't."

Her eyes widened. "Is Ginger okay?"

I glanced up at Bessie.

"She's been taken to a special hospital in Atlanta. She's going to be there a while," Bessie lied.

"Oh, that's awful."

Praise be the magicals! Stella didn't remember a thing. She started the morning off almost exactly like she had the day I all but ruined our friendship. I glanced over at Bessie, who smiled. Warmth poured over my soul and wrapped its soft security around me like a cozy knit blanket.

"Mr. Charming sees all. Mr. Charming sees all," the green parrot said.

Stella flipped around and eyed him suspiciously. "What's that about?"

I smiled. "He must have watched a psychic movie or something, right, Bessie?"

"He sure did," she said, and added a wink just for me.

Britney and Amber pranced in, giggling and laughing like they didn't know what happened.

I realized then I'd sent Atlas off to a safe place and hadn't brought him back. "Excuse me," I said. "I forgot something in my apartment."

Stella jumped up. "Let me get it for you."

I squeezed her shoulder with my good hand. "No, it's okay. I need to do things for myself." I smiled at the two young witches and whispered, "My apartment, please."

They rushed out without a word and beat me to my door.

"Witches are talking," Britney said. "Is it true?"

"Depends on what you've heard."

"That you sent that witch and her creepy old sister to where the bad witches go."

I pressed my lips together. "Let's just say you're no longer a trio. Oh, and neither of you need to involve yourself with Atlas, okay?"

They giggled.

"No, I'm serious. Just walk away. If you don't, I'll make sure you do."

Their eyes widened. "Yes, ma'am," they said in unison.

"Now, go get your lattes and tip big. Bessie deserves it."

They rushed away and I chuckled to myself. It was kind of cool being that feared and respected older person for a change.

I STOOD inside my apartment and waved my hand.

Atlas appeared in front of me. He was so surprised he lost his balance and fell onto the couch. "Oh, hey."

I raised my good hand and shook my finger at him. "No. You don't get to be all casual."

He furrowed his brow. "I...what?"

I exhaled. "I don't have the energy to get into it right now. Just do me a favor, will ya? Stay away from Britney and Amber."

"I don't want them. I want Emma."

"Yeah, I bet you do, but that's not going to happen. Emma's gone, and she's not coming back. Oh, and I know who you are." I pointed two fingers at my eyes and then at him. "And I'm watching you. You got that? One screw-up and—" I made a slash across my neck. "You understand?"

"I do," he said.

"Now go help Bessie. I have a feeling the Enchanted is going to be very busy today."

I gave him some time to get there before following. Bessie had a fresh cup of coffee waiting.

"Thank you," I said.

"Everything all right?" she asked.

"It is now."

Daisy and Cassie walked in, their arms hooked together like the best friends they were again. Their two rat familiars followed closely at their sides.

"Oh my gosh!" Stella screamed. "They brought in rats!"

I tried not to laugh, but Stella was such a drama queen sometimes. Not that I hadn't been the exact same way, but she didn't know that. "Chill, girl. Those are their pets. I was a little freaked out at first too, but they're trained, and you'd be surprised at how well behaved they are." I'd said that last part for the rodents.

Cassie and Daisy both smiled.

"Don't worry, Stella, we won't be here long," Daisy said. She smiled at Cassie and leaned her head on her shoulder. "We came to say goodbye before we head on our retreat."

"And get coffees to go," Cassie said.

"That too," Daisy agreed.

"Retreat?" Stella asked.

Cassie smiled. "We're taking an extended vacation together to make up for lost time."

"What about your stores?" she asked.

"My niece came in to work at mine until we're back," Daisy said. "She majored in retail management and social media marketing. She's already got something called a 'campaign' online and she's built a website for me. She swears it's going to bring in all kinds of new business."

"That's wonderful," I said, and meant it. "But what about your place?" I asked Cassie.

"I'm closed for now, but I'm not worried. I have a feeling once we're back, business will easily pick up." She winked at me.

We chatted for a bit longer, my smile glowing with joy for the two friends who'd spent hundreds of years hating each other because someone manipulated them into thinking they couldn't trust each other. So much time wasted for nothing.

Before they left, they both hugged me.

Cassie whispered, "You're now the Good Witch of the South."

"I wouldn't go that far," I said, but I secretly loved the title.

"We would," Daisy said.

I just hoped my friendship with Stella never had to take a break like theirs.

ANOTHER WITCH BITES THE DUST

Being a witch is complicated. Our powers have limits, and as a newer witch, I'm still getting used to what I can and cannot do. In a perfect witchy world, that works like a charm. But the witchy world isn't perfect. Not at all.

Witches don't always follow the rules, and when they don't, bad things happen in their cozy towns. Bad things like murder. Cassandra Bloom's murder, for starters.

Cassandra Bloom was the bad witch in every fairytale, the one with the ugly wart and long, stringy gray hair, taunting everyone as she flew on her broom over town. But she didn't just look scary. She was scary.

Holiday Hills residents, magical and humans, were afraid of Cassandra.

Sure, everyone in town might feel secretly relieved she's no longer with us, but they're missing the bigger picture.

Cassandra didn't die of old age. She was murdered.

The cute police chief is doing what he can, but I can't let my boyfriend not catch a killer, can I? Nope. He's struggling, so now I've got to figure out the why, how, and who, before the killer strikes again.

Because until I do, no one in Holiday Hills is safe, especially not us witches.

Click here to find out what happens!

ALSO BY CAROLYN RIDDER ASPENSON

Upgraded for Murder

The Midlife in Castleberry Paranormal Cozy Mystery Series

Get Up and Ghost

Ghosts Are People Too

Praying For Peace

Ghost From the Grave

Deceased and Desist

Déjà Boo

Haunting Hooligans: A Chantilly Adair Novella

The Pooch Party Cozy Mystery Series

Pooches, Pumpkins, and Poison

Hounds, Harvest, and Homicide

Dogs, Dinners, and Death

The Witches of Holiday Hills Cozy Mystery Series

There's a New Witch in Town

Witch This Way

Who's That Witch?

Another Witch Bites the Dust

Hungry Like the Witch

Witchy Wonderland

Witch or Without You (Coming Soon!)

Let's Hear it for the Witch (Coming Soon!)

The Midlife Psychic Medium Series

Formerly The Angela Panther Mystery Series

Unfinished Business

Unbreakable Bonds

Unbinding Love Novella

Uncharted Territory

The Ghosts Novella

The Christmas Elf Novella

Unexpected Outcomes

Undetermined Events Novella

The Event Novella

The Favor Novella

Undesirable Situations

Uncertain Circumstances

Untrue Accusations

The Garland Ghoul

Unclear Messages (Coming Soon!)

The Magical Real Estate Mystery Series

Spooks for Sale

A Haunted Offer

Other Books

Mourning Crisis

Join Carolyn's Newsletter List and receive special downloads, sales, and other exciting authory things here.

ACKNOWLEDGMENTS

Thank you to my readers, Pam, Janice, Lynn, each of you. I appreciate you.

And as always, I couldn't do what I do without such an amazing husband. Jack Aspenson, you continue to create miracles in my life, and I'm so glad you've stuck around.

ABOUT THE AUTHOR

USA Today Bestselling Author Carolyn Ridder Aspenson writes cozy mysteries, thrillers, and paranormal women's fiction featuring strong female leads. Her stories shine through her dialogue, which readers have praised for being realistic and compelling.

Her first novel, Unfinished Business, was a five-star Reader's Favorite, a Rone Award finalist, and a number one bestseller on both Amazon and Barnes and Noble. In 2021, she introduced readers to detective Rachel Ryder in Damaging Secrets. Overkill, the third book in the Rachel Ryder series, was one of Thrillerfix's best thrillers of 2021.Reviews have praised her work as *'compelling, and intense,'* and *'read through the night, edge of your seat thrillers'*.

Prior to publishing, she worked as a journalist in the suburbs of Atlanta where her work appeared in multiple newspapers and magazines. She wrote a monthly featured column in Northside Woman magazine.

Writing is only one of Carolyn's passions. She is an avid dog lover and currently spoils two pit bull boxer mixes. She lives in the mountains of North Georgia as an empty nester with her husband, a cantankerous cat, and those two spoiled dogs. You can chat with Carolyn on Facebook at Carolyn Ridder Aspenson Books or through her website at www.carolynridderaspenson.com

https://bookhip.com/MZZXKKD

Printed in Great Britain
by Amazon